Frank Samuel Child, J. Randolph Brown

The House With Sixty Closets

A Christmas Story for Young Folks and Old Children

Frank Samuel Child, J. Randolph Brown

The House With Sixty Closets
A Christmas Story for Young Folks and Old Children

ISBN/EAN: 9783743395183

Manufactured in Europe, USA, Canada, Australia, Japa

Cover: Foto ©Andreas Hilbeck / pixelio.de

Manufactured and distributed by brebook publishing software (www.brebook.com)

Frank Samuel Child, J. Randolph Brown

The House With Sixty Closets

ALL ABOUT IT

IV

V

E

LIST OF ILLUSTRATIONS.

9

A

HOUSE, PEOPLE, THINGS

I will first describe the house.

Then I will tell something about the people that live in it.

After that I will speak of the very strange things which happened there the night before Christmas.

B

THE HOUSE THAT THE JUDGE BUILT

THE HOUSE THAT THE JUDGE BUILT.

ONCE upon a time there lived a good Judge in an old New England town. People said the reason that he was so good was because his father was a minister. But he may have gotten his goodness from his mother. I don't know. Or he may have had it from his uncle who took him into his family and sent him to college. For the minister was poor, and like many of his brethren he had a big family; so his brother who was a rich lawyer and a statesman helped his nephew get his education.

Now, this son of a minister and nephew of a

great man studied law and became a Judge. He
was liked by every one who knew him. People
felt that he was an honest, noble man who had
mastered all the law books, and showed more
common sense than any other person in the State.
So they made him Judge. This man who started
poor and had to make his own way in the world
earned a great deal of money. People came to
him from all parts of the country, and sought
his advice. They put into his hands the most
important law cases. Only sometimes he would
not have anything to do with the cases that he
was asked to manage because he thought them
wrong.

As years went by he saved his money, and the
time came when he was ready to build a house.
The Judge had become the most honored and the
best known man in the State. He had many
friends among the great people of the land. He
enjoyed company, and was a famous host. So it
seemed well to him and his wife that they build
a house which should be large enough to hold

their friends, and fine enough to satisfy the taste of the society in which they moved.

The Judge was not moved by pride or a wish to make a show. He wished to do the right thing. Everybody said that he ought to have the largest and the finest house in town. He was not only a lawyer and rich, but he was deacon in the church and the leading man in society. He was likewise a great scholar; and many people said that he was the most eloquent speaker of his State. Such a person must live in a generous way. So the Judge built this house.

Now, when it came to drawing plans the wife had a good deal to say about it; for the house was to be her home just as much as his; and he always tried to do what he knew was for the pleasure of his wife. "I think," said she when they began to talk about building, "that it should have a great many closets." Had you been a friend of Mrs. "Judge" you would have seen why she said this. She was not only a woman who liked to have all her friends come to visit her, but she was also very liberal and kind. She was always doing some nice thing for people, and always giving presents.

She was able to do this because she had the things to give away. I know men and women who would make a great many presents if they had the money to buy them — at least they say that they would. Such people like to tell how they would act if they had all the money that some neighbor has saved. They are great on giving away things that do not belong to them.

Now, the Judge's wife was the best giver in town; and she gave to her friends, and the poor, and everybody that was in need, all sorts of things. But in order to do this she must buy the gifts that she scattered so freely; and when she bought things she wanted a place to keep them until the time came for her to give them away. This was why she spoke to the Judge about the closets.

"Well, my dear," said the Judge (he was always kind and polite), "you may have just as many closets as you wish." So she began her plans of the house by drawing the closets. I don't know exactly how she managed to arrange

it on paper. Very likely she said to herself, "I shall want thirty closets." And then she would divide the number into four parts and say, "Let me see, I suppose that four will be enough for the cellar. Then I shall need ten on the first floor, and twelve on the second floor, and six in the attic. That makes—why, that makes thirty-two. Dear me! I wonder if that will be enough?" And as she thinks over the various uses to which she will put her closets, and the many things she will store in them, she says, on the next day, " Well, I believe that I must have five or six more closets." So she starts her drawing by marking down thirty-eight closets. After she has settled it that the main floor shall have thirteen of them, she puts upon the paper some dots showing the size of each little room; then she draws the other rooms about them, and so she gets one story arranged.

But no sooner does she begin the plans for the next floor, than she thinks of one or two more closets which she needs for the first, and so goes back to her work of yesterday, and does it all over again, making several changes. And so very likely the weeks are spent in making paper closets, and drawing the halls and parlors and bedrooms and other rooms about them, until she puts her plans by the side of the Judge's plans; then they get an architect; and then she asks for four more closets, which makes forty-four.

After a time the men begin to build; and she sends for the builder, and tells him of course that she finds she will certainly need five more closets, — one in the cellar, two on the first story, and three on the second. He is a pleasant man; and the changes are made. But ere the house is half built other needs appear, and Mrs. "Judge" insists upon three new closets, which make fifty-two. And without doubt on the very week that the carpenters leave the handsome mansion, she asks them for several changes and three closets more. And will you believe it, they move into the new house, get nicely settled, and everything running in good order, when the generous house-wife finds that the carpenter must come, for she still wishes five new closets, which added to the others make sixty. And so you have the house with sixty closets. It seems to me that I have made it clear how there came to be so many of these curious rooms and spaces in the Judge's house. At least you know all that I know about it; and I do not believe that ever another house was built in such a way.

But I must tell you how the house was divided. A plan of each story will be the best means of fixing this in the mind; and then you can turn back to it whenever you lose your way in the house, and wish to get what are called "your bearings." We must begin at the bottom and work toward the top. The cellar was really three cellars, — a big one, a fair-sized one, and the wine cellar. There was a small closet in this deep, dark place where they kept certain kinds of liquor. The main cellar was divided lengthwise through the middle, and there were two closets for provisions on each side.

The main floor had twenty-seven closets. For my own part, I think that woman is a remarkable person who can invent and arrange such a number of little nooks and rooms. But if this is a mark of genius, what shall we say when it comes to keeping track of all the closets and their contents? Why, I should be obliged to carry a plan of the whole house with me, and every few minutes I should pull it out and study it. The Judge's wife was a most wonderful woman. She built her closets, and then she filled them, and then she remembered all about them and their contents. Here is the plan of the first floor. A hall through the middle. On the left as you enter is the library. There was one closet connected with this room, and a door opened into it from the northeast corner. Back of the library was the dining-room. It had three closets connected with it; doors leading to them from three corners of the room. To the left of the dining-room you passed into a side entry. Three doors opened into three large closets. The kitchen adjoined the dining-room. There was one closet in it, and two closets out of it to the right, and these two latter had one closet and two closets respectively.

On the right of the hall was the parlor. It had one closet. A large window reaching to the floor gave entrance to this room near the northeast corner. Back of the parlor was a long, dark

closet which made a passage-way from the hall to the schoolroom. Back of this closet was a first-floor chamber with three closets. The third of these closets opened into the chamber from the north. It was formerly Mrs. "Judge's" storeroom. Another large closet was connected with it, and these two large closets contained two small closets. To the east of this chamber was the schoolroom (formerly the Judge's library). This room had two closets in it, and two closets out of it. The room to the north of the schoolroom was the annex to the Judge's library, and it held his books bequeathed to the minister. It also held two closets. And now my first story is ended.

The short hall on the second floor opens at the rear into a long, narrow hall. There are five chambers in this part of the house. The front room on the right as you look toward the street is the "Study," and it has two closets, one on each side of the big chimney. The two chambers back and to the left as you face the chimney are without a single closet; but the lack is made up when you pass to the other side of the house. The front chamber has two closets, one on each side of the chimney. As you pass into the one on the right (you face the chimney, remember) a door opens to the right and leads you into another large closet with a window in it. Going across this closet to the right another door opens into a big, dark closet; turning to the street and stepping back three paces you open a door into another closet; passing into this one (there is a small window in it) you open a door into the linen closet. Withdrawing from this series of small rooms, you get into the Betsey-Bartram room, and there you find on the south side two doors leading into two large closets. North of this room is another bedroom. One closet lies in the southeast corner, and one opens to you from the west side of the room. The thirteenth closet on this floor is at the end of the back hall, and the fourteenth is by the side of the chimney in the room above the down-stairs chamber. The attic was one big room with five closets scattered around the chimneys. They hung hams in the larger one. It was a fine place to smoke meat. There was always a greasy, smothered flavor to the air in that place.

Now, if you have kept track of the closets you will see that we number only fifty-one. There had been three neat, retired little closets under the stairs in the first-floor hall. When the hall was enlarged these poor things were taken out. It was on this occasion that Samuel said: "See how rich we are; for we have closets to burn." And still there are six closets missing. Well, the closet with the skeleton in it is a mystery, and I do not like to speak of it. Three closets were found one day carefully tucked away in a corner of the attic. The other two missing ones have simply grown up and become big rooms with windows in them. They put on a good deal of style, and look down upon the other closets.

What a lovely time the Judge's wife had in furnishing her new home. I have been reading the bills, yellow-stained and time-worn. She had a taste for handsome things. As the house was a colonial building, the grandest in that part of the country, she tried to get furniture that matched.

There were mahogany chairs and tables, sofas

and bedsteads, cabinets and stands. She paid $155 in gold for her gilt-framed looking-glass, which stood between the front windows in the parlor, and $125 for her Grecian sofa with cushions. There were twelve fancy-chairs and two arm-chairs. Her rocker cost $25. Then she had another little work-table, for which they paid $20.75.

Her parlor carpet was made in England. The Judge had it made to order; so you may believe it was uncommonly fine. The curtains were yellow damask, lined with chintz. During the summer these curtains were stored away on long shelves in one of the closets, and lace curtains hung in their places.

Every large room in the house had a fireplace, and the supply of andirons was enormous. Some of them cost $19 and $20. Then there were venetian blinds in the parlor; and on the centre table stood an astral bronzed lamp worth $18, and on the mantle, high silver candlesticks. A plated pair cost them $18, and the snuffers and tray $8 more.   There were the best Brussels carpets, the most fashionable china and silver, the richest linen for the table, — a vast amount of things needed to make a house pleasant and comfortable.

C.

THE PEOPLE WHO LIVE IN THE HOUSE THAT THE JUDGE BUILT.

C.

THE PEOPLE WHO LIVE IN THE HOUSE THAT THE JUDGE BUILT.

T was on this wise that the present family came to live in the parsonage. The church had been without a pastor for several months, and the people were tired of hearing Tom, Dick, and Harry in the pulpit. But what was to be done? They had found no man that suited them. One minister was too young, and another too old. The first candidate had a very long neck, a sort of crane neck, and it made some of the ladies nervous. The last candidate was fat, and everybody said he must be lazy. Several were so anxious to come that the congregation turned against them.   There was always some reason why each man was not liked. So it began to look as if they might never get another minister.

The society finally asked the ladies their views upon the subject.   It was one afternoon when the Dorcas Daughters were sewing for the poor.   The president of the little band had been reading a missionary letter.   "Well," she said, "I have heard so much about filling the pulpit that I am sick of it.   I think it's about time that we filled the parsonage.   Just see what kind of ministers we have had for the last thirty years. Two bachelors, and one married man without a chick or a child.   I say that it's time for us to call a man to fill the parsonage."

"Why, that's what I think!" remarked one of the mothers present.   "It is a shame to have that great house given over to the rats and mice.   And I know that not a minister has been in it for all these years that used more'n half or two-thirds of the room.   But, dear me, it would take a pretty big family to fill the parsonage! Let me see; there are twenty-seven rooms and sixty closets, aren't there?"

"So they say," replied the president. "I never counted them. But that would just suit some folks."

"Where is that letter that you read us at the last meeting?" inquired one of the sisters. "How many children did that man say he had? I remember that we never sent another box like it to a home missionary in all the history of this church." "I've got the letter right here in my hand," said the president, "and I've had that man in mind for a week. He's got fifteen children, — eight of his own, and seven of his deceased sister. I shouldn't wonder if he was the very one we want." One of the younger women nodded. She was thinking of playmates for her boys and girls. "And then if they overflowed the house," continued the president, "there is the little building in the yard. They might start a cottage system. You know that is the way they do in schools these days. Divide up the young folks, and set them in small companies. The minister might do it; and if the family expanded we might build two or three extra cottages."

"Now, Mrs. President," said one of the ladies, "I fear you are making fun. But I think that letter from the missionary with fifteen children in the family was the best we ever had. A man that could write such a letter must be very much of a man."

"He is," replied the president. "I have looked him up in the Year Book, and I have written to the secretary of the Missionary Society. He's a very good man. Nobody has done better work in that frontier country."

So the ladies said that they would ask the church to call this parson with the big family. When the meeting was held and everybody was talking, one gentleman arose, and told the people that the ladies had a candidate. His name being proposed, the president of the Dorcas Society explained how she felt, that they ought to have a man to fill the parsonage, and this man whom they named was the one to do it; therefore the meeting voted unanimously to call him.

"I think we had better charter a train to bring them from the West," said one of the deacons. But it was finally decided to engage a car; so everything was arranged, and in four weeks they came.

When the train stopped at the station, the church committee was on hand with three carry-alls. It reminded one of an orphanage, or a company of Fresh-air children. But a hearty welcome was given; they were hurried into the carriages, and soon the whole family was in the parsonage.

A nice dinner had been prepared by the ladies of the parish. After the travellers had washed and made some slight changes, they all sat down to the feast.

It was a happy thing that the church and the Judge furnished the parsonage. This poor, large-hearted missionary brought nothing with him but books and children; his library was really a very fine one, and it had filled the small house in the West. His own family of children had been increased by the seven orphans left when his sister and her husband died. There was nothing for him to do but adopt them; so they had been packed into the little home until one was reminded of a box of sardines. But this sort of kindness was like the good man. He was ready to share the last crust with any one who needed it.

"Why, what a big house it is!" exclaimed Grace. "Just see; I guess we could put the whole of our Western house right here in the parlor." And I think they could if they had only brought it along with them. When dinner was over the children scattered all through the mansion and the grounds.

What a delightful sense of freedom and importance they had. Could it be possible that all these things belonged to them? Were the ten acres of lawn, garden, orchard, field, and pasture

really for their use and pleasure? As parents
and children wandered through the big rooms,
and peered into the sixty closets, and looked out
of the numerous windows, it seemed to them like
a dream. And yet the dreamy sensation soon
passed; for the parson and his wife, happening to
look out of a front window, were struck with
the expression of alarm, amusement, or interest
shown by several people going along the street.
It was caused by the way in which the family
was showing its presence and possession. There
were three children on the front piazza standing
in a row gazing at the sea; four of the younger
ones were climbing in and out of the windows
on the second floor, running along the tin roof
of the piazza; two boys had already climbed a
tree looking for birds' nests; three children had
hurried through the attic to the roof, and leaned
against the big chimneys that towered over the
house. With curious interest they were taking
a general survey of the town and country, quite
unconscious that their rashness attracted any at-

tention. The other youngsters were having a
frolic in the yard, walking along the top of the
picket-fence, jumping from one gate-post to another, shouting with healthful lungs, and making
the very welkin ring.

Had a pack of wild Indians swooped down
upon the house, they could not have made themselves more evident, or excited any greater con-
cern in town. It was clear that the minister
who was called to fill the parsonage answered
the purpose. He filled it; and the contents were
overflowing from doors and windows on to piazzas
and roofs, or into yard and trees and street.
What a waking up for the rats and mice it was!
The mere racket and clatter were enough to drive
them out of their holes. But what a shaking
up for the old town!

The house stood on the main street. It was
an object of historic veneration. Everybody knew
all about it, and had a sort of watch-care over
it. Anything that went on in that house belonged to the whole neighborhood. So that it

was not long before all the people were talking
about the new arrivals.   Men, women, and children felt an impulse to walk or ride by the
parsonage on that eventful day.   And it was
a startling sight; for the minis-
ter's family seemed to think that
the house really belonged to them,
and they were to en-
joy it just the way
they pleased.   This
running all through
the many rooms, and
popping out of the
many windows upon
the piazza, and climb-
ing up to the roof,
and playing tag in the

yard, and hunting for birds' nests, and walking
on the tops of the pickets along the fence, was
their way of enjoying the place.

"Let's nail the flag to the chimney," shouted
Harry, the third boy.   They had carried the flag

in hand all through their journey from the West. "Yes," shouted the other boys, who were wildly patriotic. "Come on! come on!" So they all came on except the youngest; and she finally came in the arms of her father, who followed the mother, who followed the children, to see what was doing in the attic or on the roof. And just at this time the most important man in the church and town drove by with his family. Do you wonder that this important man and his family gazed with surprise and alarm at the sight? There on the roof of the house was the whole family. Henry was nailing the flag to the tallest chimney. But when the children saw this kind man pass along the street (he was one of the committee that met them at the station, and it was his horses that had carried them to the parsonage), they waved their hands, and shook their handkerchiefs, and shouted "Hurrah! hurrah!" with such spirit that the gentleman must needs take off his hat, smile and bow, and turn to his family with some pleasing remark. There was no doubt in his mind or in the mind of the passer-by that the town was captured. The West had made a sudden onset; and the standard of victory now floated from the chimney of the Judge's mansion. The only thing for the natives to do was to submit and make the best of the situation.

As I said, the good people of the parish furnished the parsonage. The carpets were down, and the chairs, tables, sofas, bedsteads, stands, bookcases, and other things, were put in their places. All the minister's wife had to do was to unpack her trunks, and divide up their contents among the closets. All the minister had to do was to unpack his boxes, and arrange his books in the study. So they were settled in a trice.

Here is the picture of the children. You must know them in order to understand what happened in the house. Elizabeth was the oldest. She must have been seventeen or eighteen. She was ready for college. It was hard for the mother to get along without her, since she had brought up

all the younger ones, and given her mother a
chance to go round with her father in his work.
Elizabeth was very mature, but she had all the
frankness and cordiality of a typical Westerner.
She seemed almost too free and easy in her manners for the slow East. But you couldn't help

liking her. A little Western gush does good in
the town.

Samuel came next. He knew everything: He
was ready for college too. He was slow, and not
always just as agreeable as one would like to have
him. It has been said that somebody stepped on
his toes when he was a very little child, and that
he still has spells of being angry about it.

Samuel was a mechanic. He kept things in order, — machines, carts, clocks, and like objects, — when he hadn't any girls to tease; for he was an awful tease, and so was liked in a general way by all of them. His manner toward the younger members of the family was rather severe and overbearing. But what would you expect from a big boy who knows so much, and has such a host of children to live with?

Helen was the third one. She was literary, and gave a great deal of time to books. She hated to darn stockings above all things, and would often read a story to the children, or write one for them, if she could get somebody to do her darning for her. I think she will make an author. The family hadn't been in the house one day before she said that the closets must be named. Her mother or the children would never be able to keep track of them, unless they were reduced to a system, and properly numbered like rooms in a hotel, or labelled like drugs in a store.

Henry and Miriam were twins. They were just about as unlike as you could make them, — one light and the other dark; the first lean and the second fat; he quick and she slow. And so we might go through a long list of things, and find that one was opposite to the other. For this reason they got along well together and were very happy.

Then came cousin George, who was fond of music and could sing like a lark; and Theodora, who was born to be a lady, and always took the part of Mrs. Rothschild or Mrs. Astor in their plays; and cousin Herbert, who will be a doctor, and who was so ingenious about getting into mischief that I think he will be able to invent enough bad doses to cure the very worst sicknesses; and cousin Ethel, the pink of propriety, who never got a spot on her dress, and always said, "Will you please give me this or that?" or "Thank you," when she took anything; and cousin Grace, the demure and quiet puss who had a wonderful faculty for stirring up the whole family, and yet freeing herself from trouble; and cousin Susie, who is always sweet and good-tempered, and loves everybody; and cousin William, the precocious (I mean very smart), who will be president of the United States; and cousin Nathaniel, who was said by his brothers and sisters and cousins to be "just too cute for any-thing," flying hither and thither like a humming-bird, never two minutes in one place except when his aunt got him into his nest at night. How many does that make? Let me count them up. Have I mentioned them all but Ruth? Ruth was seven years old. She could ask more questions in five minutes than any lawyer in cross-exam-ining witnesses. And when she was tired of asking questions she would tease for more things in a second five minutes than any twenty children rolled into one. And not only would she ask the same question seventeen times at once, or tease for the same thing thirteen times without stopping, but she did it in just the same un-varying, shrill tone of voice; so that it was like

the monotonous rasping of a saw, and had a
tendency to drive a sensitive person out of his
head. How many times did the older members
of the family run from her as though she had
a contagious disease, so that they might get re-
lief from that endless asking and teasing? And
yet she had many good traits, and was certainly
very bright. If there had been some comfortable way of putting a muzzle upon talkative
and tedious children, her parents would probably
have done it; but they simply used all the pow-
ers of restraint that they had and let it go at
that. Ruth was evidently cut out for a poet or
a woman's rights speaker; for she was all the
time getting up rhymes, or talking in a high
key and impulsive way to such members of the
family as would listen to her.

When the baby came everybody said that he
must be called "The Little Judge," in honor of
the good man who gave the house to the church
for the minister.

No sooner was the family really settled than

the children began to ask about this famous
Judge. They had never lived in an old, historic
house before, and they were interested. They
knew how the Judge and his wife looked, for
their portraits hung in the east parlor. What fine
old people they must have been! If those oil
paintings did them justice they were about as
nice-looking as anybody that you see preserved
in oil in the great galleries of the world.

Whenever the children stood before the pictures,
they asked questions: Who was the Judge? what
did he do? how much of a family did he have?
did he like children? when did he die? who at-
tended the funeral? where was he buried? what
became of his things? and a hundred other questions. So the minister began to read about the
Judge and his work. And the more he read, the
more he admired and loved. The enthusiasm
which the minister showed in his attempts to learn
all he could about the generous giver of the parsonage excited the curiosity of the children to
such an extent that they begged their father and

uncle to write a book about him. Helen herself
talked about doing something of the kind.

"I've found out more things in the life of the
Judge," the minister would say; and then all
the children gathered around him just after supper, as the fire burned gayly on the hearth in his
study, and he would tell them some fresh incident,
and add a few lines to his pen portrait of the
man. So the months chased each other; and the
Judge and his wife made not only the most common topic of conversation, but they became as
real to the young people in the parsonage as the
boys and girls they met on the street. I suppose
it was because they thought and talked so much
about them that the strange things which I am
to relate happened (or didn't happen) in the house.

They had not lived many weeks in the house
before they got into all sorts of trouble about the
closets. They kept losing something, or losing
themselves, or losing the closets.

"We'll number them," suggested Herbert.

"No; let's name them," cried William. They

had all met to talk the matter over; so it was decided to do both. When names run out they would fall back on numbers.

"I feel like Adam when he named all the cattle and the fowls and the beasts," exclaimed Helen.

"We'll hang a plan of the house on each floor, and then we can refer to it without running up-and down-stairs." This was Samuel's remark. He was always for saving steps. So names were suggested, plans were drawn, every closet was given its dues, and the atmosphere was thick with Champagne, Darkest Africa, Turpentine, Leghorn, Daisy, Pansy, Violet, Rose, Panama, China, Greece, Dublin, Clementine, Serpentine, Argentine, Morocco, and other appropriate names.

D.

THE THINGS THAT HAPPENED TO THE PEOPLE WHO LIVE IN THE HOUSE THAT THE JUDGE BUILT.

I.

Portraits Walk and Talk.

I.

Portraits Walk and Talk.

I T was Christmas Eve. Excitement had reached fever heat. The children knew nothing about Christmas in the East; and their Western festivals had always been simple, for there was little money to use in buying gifts. But this year friends had remembered them, and they had also earned several dollars by various kinds of work; so that they were sure of many nice things. Had they not been buying presents for each other these ten days? and was not every closet in the house made the hiding-place for some treasure?

The nervous strain on the parents was great. Such confusion and anxiety passed words. Was it possible ever to get the house and the family settled down to plain, every-day living again?

It happened that the children had all met in the east parlor. This was the room where the pictures of the Judge and his wife adorned the wall. The two portraits hung on the right of the fireplace, you remember, just over the piano. A lamp was giving a faint light on the marble centre-table, and a cheerful wood fire was burning on the hearth. In front of the piano was the music stool.

The children were all talking. The hum and buzz of their many voices filled the room. One said, "I wonder if Santa Claus will bring me a doll;" and another said, "There is no such person as Santa Clause;" and a third said, "I want a new sled;" and a fourth said, "Father promised me a book about birds;" and so the talk continued.

But Ruth for once kept still. She was worn out with excitement. As she flung herself into a big arm-chair, she turned her head towards the fire, and began to see all sorts of funny creatures dancing in and out among the coals. Ruth was a poet, you remember, gifted with a wonderful imagination; and she could see more strange things, and tell more wild stories, than any other child in the family; and that is saying a great

deal, for they all had a way of telling about things which they had heard and seen that constantly reminded their neighbors of Western largeness and exaggeration.

As Ruth watched the queer creatures playing in the fire her eyes grew heavy; and then she turned her head away for a moment, and her eyes became fixed upon the pictures of the Judge and his wife. Did her head droop to one side, and did it fall softly upon the cushion against the arm, or did her eyes suddenly open wide with surprise, and did she gaze with startled look upon a strange scene before her?

For both the Judge and his wife seemed to be moving; and they looked so natural and pleasant when they smiled and bowed, that Ruth said to herself, "Why, they must be alive." And the Judge reached out his hand from the canvas which held him, and took the hand of his wife, who had responded to his motion, and said, "My dear, wouldn't you like to step down and out for a little while?"

"Yes, thank you," she replied; "I think it would rest me." And then he laid down the pen, which he holds in the picture, and stepped lightly upon the piano, still keeping her hand in his; and then he helped her down upon the piano, and then he stepped down to the music stool, and finally on

the floor, and she followed. This was all done with the grace and dignity that marked the usual movements both of the Judge and his wife. And it seemed the most natural thing in the world for them to step down and out.

Ruth sprang toward them on the instant that they stood upon the floor. She rubbed her eyes to make sure that she was not dreaming; and then as she saw them really before her, looking for all the world like natural folks, she greeted them with delight.

"Why, how do you do?" she exclaimed. "I always thought you looked as if you would like to talk. That, I suppose, is why people say that your pictures are a 'speaking likeness.' But I never thought you'd get out of the pictures. How did you do it?" But the Judge and his wife were too much absorbed in the scene before them to reply immediately. The old room had changed since their day; they were noting the changes. And then this roomful of children took them by surprise.

"My dear," said the Judge to his wife, "this is delightful." "Yes," continued Ruth, "they all belong to us. I heard the president of the Dorcas Society say that when the church called this minister they expected him to fill the parsonage just as much as the pulpit. And we did it."

"Yes, this is delightful," repeated the Judge. "How many are there?" He said this to his wife, but Ruth answered.

"Oh! there are only fifteen of us when we are by ourselves. There are a good many more when the neighbors' children come in; and then don't we have grand times!"

"It almost takes my breath away." Mrs. "Judge" was speaking to her husband. "My dear, have you my fan in your pocket?" And the Judge felt in his pocket, but he didn't find any fan.

"Why, it's Christmas! You don't want a fan," said Ruth, who was bound to take part in the conversation, and play the hostess on this wonderful occasion. And then the Judge and his wife stood stock-still, and gazed with increasing pleasure and interest upon the scene.

Their descent from the picture had been so

noiseless and unexpected that Ruth was the only one to observe it. But when this keen, talkative sister began to question the guests, the other children turned their heads, and they beheld the curious sight. There stood the Judge and his wife exactly as they appeared in the portraits. Only they had their legs on them, and the pictures didn't. But the children noticed even the smallest details of dress, and they were the very originals of the portraits.

Suddenly the whole company stood up.

"Why, it's just like a reception or a wedding," said Ruth. "I think they're all waiting to be introduced." And the children advanced one after another, or Ruth led the Judge and his wife to different parts of the room, and each brother and sister and cousin was properly presented.

"How did you get out?" inquired Ruth a second time. Everybody in the room was now standing, and all eyes were looking for the next move in this strange parlor drama.

"We just stepped out," replied the Judge, who

seemed prepared at length to talk with Ruth or the other children.

"But where did you keep your legs all the time?" When Ethel asked this question Mrs. "Judge" blushed. Elizabeth, the eldest daughter, pushed her way forward, and said, " S-s-s-s-h ! " and Samuel said, with a nudge of the arm, "Keep still, can't you?" But you might as well tell the steaming teakettle to stop boiling as it sits upon a lively fire.

"We are very glad to see you," interrupted Helen. She was a most hospitable girl, and she had read a great deal of history; although Henry knew more history than she did, and he had read everything about the Judge that he could lay his hands on.

"We are very glad to see you, and should like to ask about the 'Hartford Convention,'" said Henry.

"He's been talking about it for a month," continued Ruth. "I wish you'd tell him all about it, and then maybe he'd keep still. I don't care anything about it, neither do the other children. But

Henry thinks he's very smart in such things ever since he got a prize in history."

"Did you say these were all the children?" It was Mrs. "Judge" that now spoke. And as she made the inquiry Susie ran out of the parlor, and disappeared in the gloom of the hall.

"Why, we forgot all about the baby!" exclaimed Ruth. "He's up-stairs asleep, I guess. Dear me, you must see the baby. He's the cutest little thing you ever saw."

"Yes, we should like to see him, of course. We both like babies, good babies."

"Babies that don't cry I suppose you mean," said Ruth. "Well, he doesn't cry much, — only when he's hungry, or a pin sticks into him, or he gets mad, or somebody lets him fall, or hits his head against the door or a chair." Here Ruth paused for breath. Then she exclaimed, "Why, of course, you must see the baby! Why, he is named for you!" This was said to the Judge with greatest excitement. And just as Ruth was saying it everybody turned toward the door, and there stood little Susie hugging the baby to her breast, his nightdress dragging on the floor, her short arms barely reaching around his plump body; both baby and Susie having their faces wreathed in smiles. Staggering under the burden this youngest sister pressed through the company with her precious armful; and as the Judge saw her approach he stepped forward, bent ward, bent

down above her, and took **the** little fellow into his arms, where he settled with a most contented and happy expression. It was a very pretty sight, — this stately old gentleman holding a beautiful baby on one arm, and reaching over to the lovely, dignified wife by his side with the other arm;

for she had taken hold of his hand again after he had fixed the baby comfortably on his arm, and Ruth had stationed herself close by the Judge's wife on the other side, and taken possession of the lady's free hand.

"And this is the baby, is it?" inquired Mrs. "Judge." "What a dear little boy he is! And what did you say you called him?" For the lady was either deaf or absorbed so that she did not hear all that Ruth had said about the baby's name.

"Why, we call him after your husband. Didn't you hear me say so? He is the "Little Judge." Just see how he clings to his namesake. Is he the Judge's namesake or the Judge his namesake? I don't know which is which, only it's something about namesake, and he's named for the Judge." This latter talk on the part of Ruth was quite as much to herself as to the visitors. And all the time the Judge was gazing down into the infant's face with earnest, wistful look, seeming almost to forget that he was once more standing in the old east parlor. Yes, for a moment he had really

forgotten where he did stand; for he was thinking of the many years ago when two other baby
boys had been placed in his arms, and with what
hope and tenderness he had handled the small,
helpless pieces of humanity.

"Don't you like the name?" interrupted Ruth.
"We thought it would please you. What makes
you look so solemn? Oh, I know!" Now, Ruth
did not intend to be cruel. She was simply
thoughtless like many other children.

"You had a baby boy once, didn't you? Two
of 'em, didn't you?" And then she saw that Mrs.
"Judge" seemed to feel bad too, and that she let
go the Judge's hand for a moment, and dashed
away some tears from her eyes.

"I'm sorry if I've hurt your feelings," said
Ruth. "I didn't mean to. I was just thinking
about your two baby boys. They would have
been awful old if they had lived till now, wouldn't
they? and we never should have lived in this
house if they had lived, would we?" A hush had
fallen on the company. Neither the Judge nor his

wife made any reply. They were lost in thought, while the children watched them with breathless interest.

"We didn't dare give him your full name," continued Ruth. "That's what Dr. Blank did to one of his baby boys, and it died. Mother was afraid if we called our baby after you, with the three long names, that it might kill him, so she said; so we dropped the middle one, and I think it much better, don't you?"

"Dear little boy," said the Judge affectionately, as he looked down into his face again. "Dear little boy." And then the Judge bent down and kissed him, and the baby beamed with delight. It was almost like a baptism in church.

"I thought maybe you were going to pray over him. That's the way father does, you know." But the Judge didn't seem to hear.

"My dear," he said, turning to his wife and holding the baby toward her. She knew what he meant, for she likewise bent down over the little fellow and printed another kiss upon his sweet, upturned, dimpled face, and then another, and a third, while the Judge stood looking on with happy indulgence; and all the children noted every motion in this singular drama.

"What did your boys die of?" asked Ruth, who did not wish to lose any time, since she had so many questions to ask, and she feared that her visitors might not stay as long as she wished them.

"Ruth!" exclaimed Samuel, who had drawn near the young inquisitor, and felt it was time to stop her; "aren't you ashamed of yourself?" He said this in a low tone, thinking that the Judge and his wife might not hear. They were watching the baby with such eagerness that they had almost forgotten the rest of the company.

"I think," remarked Mrs. "Judge," as she lifted her head from the baby and glanced around the room, " that it is very pleasant in the old house."

"Oh, yes; we think so to." It was Ruth again speaking. The other members of the family had little chance to say anything. " Can't get in

a word edgewise," whispered Henry to Helen.
"What a perfect nuisance Ruth is!"

"Wouldn't you like to go over the house?"
Of course it was Ruth who asked the question.
She was always taking people over the house. It
might be Monday morning when everything was
in dire confusion, and all the younger children still
in bed, or it might be early evening after the baby
and Susie had been playing in crib and bed, and
things were assuming their wonted appearance of
disorder. If the notion took her she was always
ready to seize a caller by the hand, and lead him
from cellar to garret.

"I think I would like to look around a little,"
replied the lady. "I am wondering how many
closets you have now in the house."

"Oh, there is an awful lot!" exclaimed Ruth.

"We have sixty," observed Elizabeth, who liked
to be precise.

"That's right, that's right," continued Mrs.
"Judge." "I had that number put in. I was
afraid you might have given away some of

them." When she said this the children looked rather queer. Who ever heard of giving away closets? One might think they were flowers, or eggs, or peaches.

"You used to give away a great deal, didn't you?" exclaimed Ruth. "But I don't see how you could give away closets."

And now the whole company started on a tour of sight-seeing in the old house. Samuel and Elizabeth naturally took the lead, being the oldest and quite the lady and gentleman. The Judge with the baby on one arm and his wife leaning on the other followed. Ruth still clung to the right hand of Mrs. "Judge." Then the remaining children came in a dense crowd just behind them.

"The parlor looks much as it did when we left it, except the furniture," said the lady. "Now let us see if they have kept the other rooms as well."

They passed next into the hall.

"Dear me! what is this?" exclaimed the Judge. "Where are we?" For it was not the old hall

at all. That had been rather short and small.
This was long, reaching through the house.

"Why, what has become of my bedroom?"
inquired the lady. "They have made it into this
hall. And where are all the nice little closets
under the stairs? You certainly have given them
away. Oh, dear! oh, dear! I'm so sorry."

"I guess you're tired," said Ruth. "It makes
you nervous to walk much, doesn't it? Why, yes,
I know, because they say you never went up-stairs
for ever so many years. Oh, I know what we'll
do! You can ride." All this time Mrs. "Judge"
was looking about her in a dazed way, quite at
sea in respect to her surroundings. For the hall
had been completely changed until it appeared
about as different as different could be. And the
good lady was really shocked.

"Do you see those things under the stairs?
They are our bicycles."

And the Judge and his wife gazed with perplexed faces in the direction indicated. There
was a whole row of them. Seven, altogether, —

full-grown, half-grown, or any size you might wish. It was like a carriage shop.

" I think you might ride one all through the house down-stairs," said Ruth to the lady guest. " Then you wouldn't have to walk."

And as the suggestion was made, Ruth's eyes flashed, and her cheeks grew flushed with excitement. What fun it would be to push the good woman on a bicycle from room to room, and show her the present arrangements of the beloved house. But Mrs. "Judge" was horrified. She clung very closely to her husband, as if she thought that she might have to perch upon one of the machines whether she wished it or not. Her breath came fast and short. Her cheeks grew hectic.

" You don't mean to say that people ride those things!" she finally exclaimed when her first flurry of agitation was past.

" Yes," replied Ruth delightedly; " we all ride 'em."

" Not your father and mother, — the minister and the minister's wife?"

"Why, yes, and the Episcopal minister too, and his wife."

"Are you sure, Judge, that you didn't bring a fan with you?" The good woman seemed very faint, and she looked beseechingly toward her husband. "Here's one," shouted Susie, who ran to the cabinet and found a lovely piece of feather work, which scattered very fine feathers over your clothes and through the room on every motion you made with it. And as the Judge's wife waved it back and forth the feathers began to fly.

"It looks like a snow-storm," whispered Herbert to Theodora. And soon the feather flakes adorned their garments and floated through the air, so that one was really reminded of a fresh fall of snow.

It took the good lady a long time to get her breath. The hall closets were all gone; and in their places stood seven things called bicycles, upon which the minister, his wife, and the children were said to ride. It was awful. And

Ruth was urging her to try one. Alas! the hall was too much for her self-possession.

"Let us go into the west room," she said faintly. So they all came into what is now the family sitting-room and library. Here everything was strange. The door into the kitchen was covered with a high book-case filled with literature. The small cubby-hole through which dishes and food had been passed from dining-room to kitchen was now made into a door. But there was one familiar object before them. In the far corner stood the clock, grave and stalwart sentinel for the house.

"My dear, do you see the clock?" It was the Judge speaking to his wife. He knew there must be many changes in the house. He accepted them very quietly; but he was glad to see this old familiar friend. He had expected to find it in the hall where it had always stood during his day; but he was just as glad to see it here in the old dining-room. That clock had been present on all the great occasions of life.

It had marked the hours for every event connected with the history of the house. When
the long line of famous men and women enter-
tained by the Judge and his wife came to mind,
it was to be recollected that the clock had seen
them all, and winked and blinked at them morning, noon, and night, and sounded his warning
notes in their ears, when it was time to rise or
retire, or to eat, or to go to court, or to drive to
town, or to start for church. It was like meeting a tried and beloved friend. Both the Judge
and his wife were overjoyed.

It might have been that some indifferent family
had lived in the house, and thrown the clock out
of doors or stored it in the attic. There are
people so dull and unimaginative, people with so
little sentiment, that they never care for keep-
sakes or heirlooms. They want everything fresh
and new about them. Antiques are a perfect bore
or nuisance. Happily the minister's family was
not one of this kind. They all had a great deal
of what is called historic sense. They liked old

things; and the clock was their most sacred possession. How much they had talked about it, and dreamed about the scenes which had passed before it! While Ruth had invented more wild stories in connection with that one object than could be told in many a day.

The other things in the room attracted little attention. The visitors made their slow and stately way across to the corner where the clock stood. As they looked up into its serene face, the object of their interest looked down upon them with a very knowing expression, seeming to recognize them on the instant, extending them a very hearty welcome; for the tick, tick was louder than ever before, the very frame of the huge thing began to tremble with suppressed excitement, and then eight long, loud strokes sounded through the entire house, as much as to say, " They've come," " How'd do? " " Glad t'see you," and other kind greetings. The children had all followed the Judge and his wife, and they were eagerly watching for the next movement on the part of the visitors.

It made quite a striking picture,—the tall, solemn clock in
the far corner of the room, the
Judge and the baby on his arm,
and the wife holding Ruth by
the hand, standing in front
of it; then the throng of
alert and wondering chil-

dren bringing up in the rear, for they all felt
that something out of the ordinary was about to

happen. In fact, the whole visit of these former inhabitants of the house was rather unusual, so that the children would naturally expect fresh marvels at any moment. It was clear that Mrs. " Judge " was getting tired; nobody had offered her a chair, and she had refused to get on a bicycle.

Suddenly the door of the clock swung open.

" I think you had better rest, my dear," said the Judge; " we'll step in here."

And as he made the remark he put his foot into the clock and gave a lively spring, filling the small doorway.

" Oh, please don't take the baby away ! " screamed Ruth, as she saw them both disappearing. " Who'll nurse him ? And mamma'll feel so bad."

But it was all done so quickly that Ruth never finished her speech, for the Judge still held his wife's hand and helped her into the clock; then as Ruth held all the faster to the lady's hand, she was caught up too, they all went into the clock and the door shut upon them.

The other children were struck dumb with amazement.

"I always thought it looked like a coffin," exclaimed Samuel; "but I never expected to see four people buried alive in it."

"I've wanted to hide in it a hundred times," said Helen, "but I never supposed" —

"Ten thousand times are hid in it," interrupted Henry.

"Times out of mind," whispered Herbert.

"Time, time," cried Samuel; and soon they indeed had a "time."

II.

Closets Talk and Walk.

II.

Closets Talk and Walk.

HE first thing that the children who were left behind did was to examine the clock. They all made a rush for it, and pulled open the door.

"Tick, tock, tick, tock," went the huge machine. They saw the pendulum swing back and forth. And that was all they did see. The Judge, his wife, Ruth, and the baby had disappeared.

"I believe this house is bewitched, or we are!" exclaimed Helen. She had read about the strange things said and done in the old town more than two centuries ago, when witches rode through the air on broomsticks, and very lively times stirred up the people.

"It was on this very spot, I've heard father say, that one of the witches lived."

"Oh, pshaw!" cried Samuel, who knew everything; "there isn't any such thing as witchcraft. They've just stepped out for a moment, and they'll come back soon."

"I think they've stepped in," replied Henry, who stood close to the clock when their visitors disappeared with Ruth and the baby. "Let's play 'tag' while we're waiting for them to come back." This was a good way to work off their nervousness; for they were all more or less nervous, either because they really thought that the witches might be upon them, or because they would have to answer to their parents for the absence of Ruth and the baby.

"We'll start from the piano," said Samuel. It was Christmas Eve, you remember, and everything seemed rather uncommon and surprising. So they all jumped upon the piano, — thirteen of them altogether, — and it made the old instrument shiver and rattle, and try to shake them off. Then they started on the game of "tag." Samuel sprang from the piano to the cabinet, from the cabinet to the mantle, and from the ·

mantle to the glass book-case in the corner; and they all jumped after him and each other. Then he swung himself over to the hall door, for his arms and his legs were simply prodigious. From

the top of the door he leaped to the big picture
frame between the front windows. How it swayed
and creaked and screamed! So he dropped down
upon a low bookcase beneath, and balanced himself on the edges of a crystal loving-cup. But
Henry and Herbert had started in the other direction from the piano, and they came face to
face with Samuel on the loving-cup. Then this
elder brother sprang over to the marble centre-
table, and then across to the piano again, and
upon the high set of book-shelves in the south-
west corner of the room. Here he began to grab
the books, and throw them at the other children
as they came near him. Then they threw books
back at him. And what a commotion there was!
Children were passing and repassing with the
speed of the wind. They were leaping from
picture to picture, and mantle to table, and piano
to book-case, and table to chairs, and cabinet to
door; books were flying in every direction, the
piano was groaning and shaking and scolding,
and there was the din of many voices, shout-

ings, laughter, cries, boys' clothes and girls' clothes woven into a perfect mass of changing colors and shapes, the bang and rattle of moving furniture, and whatever you may be pleased to imagine.

All this time the Judge, his wife, Ruth, and the baby sat composedly behind the face of the clock, and looked down delightedly upon the hilarious scene. There was a hole in the clock's face which served them for a window. Ruth had often observed it; and she had told her mother more than a few times that she was perfectly sure there must be a big room up there, and lots of people in it, for she had seen the flash of their eyes when they peeped down into the room and watched (wouldn't it be more proper to say clocked) the people. Ruth, of course, was right; for wasn't there a big room in the top of the clock? and didn't the Judge and his wife know all about it? It was there that they had gone to rest.

The first thing they did was to put Mrs.

"Judge" to bed. This they did with her shoes on. The next thing was to get the baby to sleep. So the Judge sat down in a rocking-chair, and began to sing to his little namesake; and when he got tired of singing the Judge whistled. The baby was just as good as he could be. He laughed, and cooed, and hit the old gentleman on the cheek with a tiny hand, and tried to pick his eyes out one by one, count all his teeth, and pull off his eyebrows, dig into his ears, and find what he did with his nose, and how he kept his cravat on. Meanwhile Ruth was looking down upon the children, and reporting their doings to her visitors.

"I think it will do them good to have a little frolic," said the Judge.

"Yes, let them play," replied Mrs. "Judge." "It makes me feel as if we were once more back in the old home, and had children to fill it and bring us joy."

"But you wouldn't let your children play like that," said Ruth. "Why, I think they're going to break everything to pieces. And what will the church committee say? They have charge of the house, you know."

"Let's see what they are doing!" exclaimed the Judge. So he put the baby down by his wife while he looked through the eye of the clock. Just at that moment the children had all jumped upon the centre-table; and it was crowded with thirteen of them, and the lamp in the middle. There was a brief struggle, then the lamp went out, and the noise of a great fall and crash sounded through the room, after which darkness and silence prevailed. Something had evidently happened.

"Don't you think we might visit the closets now?" inquired Ruth. The Judge turned to his wife to see what she answered.

"I am too tired to go through them," she said. "But I should like to have them come to me." Now, this was quite an original idea; but it pleased Ruth.

"Why, yes, I think they would like to come."

Ruth was speaking with great animation. "We've named them, you know; and I think if I should call them by their names they'd all be glad to see you. Can you sit here by this hole in the clock?"

"Oh, yes!" replied Mrs. "Judge." "That would be very nice. And the closets can all pass in front of us, and I can have a little talk with them." So Ruth looked down again into the room where the children had been playing, and saw that it was quite light and the children were all gone. At once she called the closets.

"I've got a list of their names in my pocket," she explained to Mrs. "Judge." "We can't remember as you can. Even as it is, mother's all the time losing something in some of the closets, and she tries so hard to think where she puts things. She ought to carry a blank-book with her, and set everything down." The Judge's wife was rested now, so that she sat up and took her place before the hole in the clock. The baby was back again in the arms of his namesake. Then Ruth shouted out the names of the closets.

"Champagne," she cried. This was the name of the wine-closet. It was a big black hole in the main cellar, just under the parlor. Very soon there was a heavy tread in the west parlor where the clock stood, and in swung Champagne. Although such a great closet he looked very thin and dismal.

"Good-even-ing," said the Judge's wife.

"How do you do?" replied Champagne; and there was a great deal of pain in his voice.

"You don't seem happy," said Mrs. "Judge."

"I'm thirsty;" and the closet's voice sounded as if a fever had parched it. "Poor folks live

here now. They haven't put a bottle of wine
into me in forty years. I'm drying up. I shall
cave in one of these days."

"That would be dreadful, wouldn't it?" exclaimed Ruth. "Would the house go down if
the wine-cellar caved in?"

"Hope so," answered Champagne testily.
"Don't even keep wine for sick folk. Somebody did put a couple of bottles of something
into me when the children had the measles, but
somebody else came and stole it out of me. I
thought I'd help bring the measles out, but they
didn't give me a chance."

"Poor fellow!" exclaimed Mrs. "Judge." "I'm
sorry for you. But these are days of total
abstinence, you know. You mustn't expect much
wine. Don't they keep butter in you?"

"No, they don't make any. And when they
get some in the house it goes as fast as it comes.
This family eats an awful sight of butter."

"Well, I'll see what I can do for you, Champagne."

"We can fill him up with water," whispered Ruth. "For the cistern leaks now, and father says the overflow all goes into the wine-cellar. "I'll call 'Greece' next." Champagne stepped one side, and stood by the front door.

"Greece, Greece." The name was spoken with shrill, positive tones; and Greece came hurrying down-stairs. This closet was in the attic. They smoked the hams in him, and they sometimes put bacon and dried beef up there.

"How do you get along?" inquired Mrs. "Judge," as the closet shambled into the west room.

"How'd' do, ma'am?" There was a strong smell of ham when Greece made his appearance.

"I've mostly given up smoking these days. I'm a poor, ham-sick fellow. They are trying to starve me to death. I haven't had anything in me for months. They won't let me say anything. They shut me up all the time."

"I think Greece smells bad, don't you?" said

Ruth as she turned to her guest. And then Ruth put her thumb and forefinger up to her nose to keep out the bad odors that seemed to come up from poor Greece. "I'm going to call 'China.'" So Greece stepped one side without one kind word. "China, China, China." There was a very loud rattling of dishes, jingling of glasses, and much music, as the long closet between the kitchen and the dining-room stepped briskly before them.

"I'm glad to see you," said the Judge's wife by way of greeting. She was a lover of fine ware, and the house had been filled with it.

"I'm very glad to see you," replied China. "I am living a wretched life."

"Dear me, don't talk like that!" exclaimed the good lady, much annoyed at all this mourning and fault-finding.

"I guess you'd talk worse than that if you had been cut down, torn to pieces, burnt up, and boxed as I have been. Don't you see that there is hardly anything left of me? As likely as not to-morrow they'll set to work and do something else to me,—make me smaller yet, or drive me out of the house. I can't tell what a day will bring forth. And just look at the dishes. Did you ever see such a lot of nicked, broken, mismatched, cracked, blackened, ugly old ware as they keep on my shelves? It makes me sick. I wish you'd come back." All this time China had been talking in a most despondent tone, giving a fresh shake of discontent to the curious assortment of ware displayed on the shelves. It made the Judge's wife nervous. She didn't like it. Neither did Ruth. It was not what they expected. Such talk was hardly in keeping with Christmas Eve.

"China, you just go right out-doors and wait in the cold," said Ruth. "I'm going to call 'Panama.' That, you know, is the closet that connects father's study right over this room with the bedroom behind it. Come, Panama," she cried. There was a great rustling of papers, and dust filled the room as Panama entered.

"What does this mean?" inquired Mrs. "Judge," who began to sneeze and feel very thirsty.

"Why, this is the closet where father keeps his sermons. I think they must rustle and make so much noise because they are dry."

"Good-evening," said the lady in the clock as she bowed.

"Good-evening," replied Panama. "It's a long time since we've seen you, Madam. Have you come back to stay?" And one could detect anxiety in the manner and speech.

"Oh, no! We are here just for the evening. We thought it would be pleasant to step down and out for a little while. We were in the portraits on the east parlor wall, you remember. When the wind gets in the east we shall be obliged to go back." Then Panama began to cry; and as fast as he cried he drank up his tears.

"I don't see what's got into the closets to make them talk so and act so!" exclaimed Ruth. "They

just seem bent on being disagreeable to-night.
And I thought we'd have such a nice time with
them. They're a discontented and complaining
lot. I'm going to call 'Leghorn.'"

During this little talk the Judge's wife was
lost in thought. Her chin had dropped down
upon her breast, and a far-away look appeared
in her eyes.

"Leghorn, Leghorn, come here!" shouted Ruth.

The children had given this name to the east-
corner closet in Mrs. "Judge's" bedroom. She
used to keep her bonnets there. One of them
was a white, beautiful Leghorn, which cost more
than twenty-five dollars. This closet was full of
shelves, and it proved very useful to the minister's
family.

"Good-evening," said the lady.

Leghorn looked up with surprise. He recog-
nized her voice.

"How do you do? When did you come?
What's the news?" Leghorn spoke in a very
familiar way; for he had always stayed close to

the head of the bed in the room, and overheard
all the conversation between the Judge and his
wife.   There was no better informed closet in
the house than Leghorn.

"You look quite cheerful," said the lady.

"Yes'm," he replied; "I keep very busy, and
have really more than I can 'tend to.   You know,
we have a perfect crowd of girls here in the house,
and their hats just fill me up to the brim.   Hear
'em fuss as I shake 'em."   And as the folks in
the clock listened they heard such a racket of
straw and such a shrill chirping that they were
quite startled.

"Dear me, what is that queer noise?" inquired
Mrs. "Judge."   "Have you a flock of birds inside
of you?"

"Oh! I know what that is," explained Ruth.
"I can hear it above the rustling of the straw.
It's all the birds we have had on our hats.   They
are feeling so good.   For we have joined the
Audubon Society, and we can't wear any more
birds.   How they flutter and sing, don't they?"

"You don't mean that you really wear whole birds on a hat or a bonnet, do you?" One could tell from the way she spoke that the visitor was horrified.

"Why, yes; and you ought to see folks come to church with them. I've counted seventeen kinds of feathers and nine pieces of birds on the girls and ladies while father was preaching his sermon. We've had a bird-class here, you know, and I can tell a great deal about 'em. There was a blackbird and there was a bluebird; and one lady had a hawk's wing, and another a rooster's tail, and Elizabeth had the breast and beak of a scarlet tanager, and Helen wore heron's feathers, and mother had ostrich plumes; and you ought to see the beautiful plumage we took from a wild turkey sent us from the West; and we put it on Susie's hat, and it was just too lovely for anything. But we've all joined the Audubon Society now, and can't kill any more birds or wear many feathers."

"I'd like to join too," interrupted Leghorn.

"I'm sick of birds in me. They make such a noise, and keep me stirred up all the time, so I don't get good sleep. I'm very nervous, but I'm quite happy."

" There, we've found one happy closet anyway," said Ruth. " You just sit down here and make yourself comfortable."

"Darkest Africa next," shouted Ruth. This was another of the closets connected with the down-stairs bedroom. He came stumbling and grumbling along.

" What do you want ? " he said in a grumpy, disagreeable way. " You've kept me in the dark so long, I've lost the use of my windows."

" Well, you needn't be so cross about it," answered Ruth. " Don't you see it's Mrs. ' Judge ' that's come back to see you ? "

" What ? what ? " cried Darkest Africa, rubbing his eyes and speaking in his natural voice. " Where is she ? "

" Why, up here in the clock, of course. Haven't you any sense ? "

"Oh, such a life as we're living!" he said, turning toward the visitor.

"You remember how you used to keep all your groceries in me, and how my shelves were heavy with every good thing,—tea, coffee, spices, fruits, and a thousand things. Well, now they've shut the blinds, and covered the windows, and turned me into a photograph-room. It's very nasty. Bad smells hang all about me. Stove-pipe, pans of dirty water, chemicals, and I don't know what, make me very unhappy. And the children run through your bedroom just as if it were a public street. Such goings on you never did see. I want to leave this world."

"I'm ashamed of you to talk that way, Darkest Africa. You go out on the piazza, and wait in the cold, too, until I call you. Such talk makes Mrs. 'Judge' feel real bad." And this closet withdrew, still mumbling about his troubles.

"I'm going to call three together now," said Ruth; "for the baby'll wake up before we get through, if I don't hurry." The Judge had really sung and whistled the baby to sleep; and there the good man sat on the edge of a cog-wheel, holding the little fellow in his arms.

"Come, 'Pride,' 'Vanity,' and 'Ophir,'" screamed Ruth. One of these closets held the clothes of the older girls — that was Pride; Vanity was filled with the many dresses of the younger girls; and Ophir was the closet where the present family kept their small stock of valuables, like jewelry, silverware, and family heir-looms. These three closets came prancing down together, and they certainly felt good. It was

Christmas Eve, and they knew it, for they were running over with all sorts of packages; their shelves were filled; their hooks were burdened with garments; the very floors were piled high with stuff. Mrs. "Judge" did not know them so well by night, for she hadn't visited them for many years before her going away. She bowed to them, and they bowed to her; but they kept their hands in their pockets.

" Why don't you say something ? " It was Ruth's remark to them as they stood in a row before the clock.

" We're waiting for you to say something first," was the reply.

" How do you feel? " This was by way of starting the conversation.

" We feel jolly. Don't you? " Mrs. "Judge" smiled. This was pleasant to hear, and she was very cheerful. She could see thirty-seven or fifty dresses. There were all sizes, colors, materials, and patterns. Their brightness and variety fascinated her.

" Look here, my dear," she said, turning to her husband.

" I can't. I should wake the baby," and he smiled in a very happy, dignified way.

"I'll call ' Morocco,' too," said Ruth. "There's plenty of room, and I like to see them together."

"Morocco, Morocco." And then there was such clattering and pattering of shoes that it seemed as if the baby must wake up; for Morocco was the shoe closet, and there were so many pairs of old shoes in the place that it reminded one of a cobbler's shop. There were little shoes and big, slippers and rubber-boots, patent leathers and copper toes, high-heeled shoes and no-heeled shoes; there were blacking and brushes and shoe-strings and button-hooks and dirt. And as Morocco walked in, every shoe and boot and slipper and brush was in a most frolicsome mood, jumping hither and thither, knocking the sides of the closet, and raising a great dust. The Judge's wife looked from Pride to Vanity, then from Ophir to Morocco. As the clothes shook and rustled, as the silver and the old-fashioned jewelry jingled, as the foot-gear banged and rattled, Ruth began to sing and dance, and the lady nodded her head to keep time; and then the Judge caught the movement and beat time with his foot, and whistled an old tune; and then the baby woke up, clapped his hands, and cooed with delight.

But time was passing very quickly, and there was a great deal to do before midnight came or the east wind arose. So Ruth hurried the closets along in their march before the guests.

"'Valentine,' 'Argentine,' 'Serpentine,' 'Clementine,' and 'Turpentine,' come along with you," she shouted urgently. These were the five closets which belonged to the Judge's library. Valentine had nothing but broken furniture in him; Argentine was loaded down with old and useless silver (plated ware) and like stuff; Serpentine contained aged newspapers and magazines; Clementine was pretty well filled with a variety of dolls, and they played merrily as the closet came into the room, and stood first on one foot and then on the other; Turpentine brought a good deal of dust with him. He used to hold the Judge's private papers. They were dry as dust. The Judge was so interested in the baby that he paid no attention to the closets.

"I'm going to call the closet with the skeleton in it," whispered Ruth. "We named him the 'Wandering Jew;' we've never seen him, you know. Somebody told us that the key was lost, and then the keyhole, and finally the closet itself, and it must be so; for where that closet was in your day there isn't anything now." During this remark Mrs. "Judge" looked very restless and sorrowful. "I just want to see what a skeleton in the closet is like. I've heard that every family has got one, but they keep them out of sight. Wandering Jew, Wandering Jew," whispered Ruth with surpressed excitement; and almost on the instant the lost closet walked into the room from nowhere. He was quite small; as he walked something rattled in him. The child shivered. Was it the skeleton? and would she see it? Then she remembered that the key and the keyhole were both lost.

"What's in it?" whispered Ruth. And then she noticed for the first time that the lady was weeping. There was a strange silence. Mrs.

"Judge" put her hands upon Ruth's head, and looking down pathetically into her eager eyes said gently, "I would rather not put any questions to the Wandering Jew, or try to make him say anything. Let him pass along out of my sight." And Ruth, who was quite awed by the grief of Mrs. "Judge," told the closet to hurry out of sight as soon as possible. So she never knew whether it was blasted hopes or withered love, or the ghost of a chance or the dry bones of scholarship, or something else that was locked in that strange little haunted room.

And now the closets were hurried along as fast as Ruth could name them. But Mrs. "Judge" seemed to have lost her interest. The closet with a skeleton in it had thrown her off her balance. She had little or nothing to say to any of the others; and Ruth herself grew tired, so that she was very glad when they had all made their bows and said their short say, and something else might be done for the entertainment of her company.

III.

THE PROCESSION OF
GOAT,
DOG,
CAT,
BICYCLES,
PORTRAITS,
RUTH,
AND
THE "LITTLE JUDGE."

III.

THE PROCESSION OF GOAT, DOG, CAT, BICYCLES, CLOSETS, PORTRAITS, RUTH, AND THE "LITTLE JUDGE."

THINK it would be real nice for us to take a little ride about the town, don't you?" Ruth was speaking to the Judge and his wife.

"Yes, I think I am rested enough to go a short way," was the lady's reply. "But what shall we do with the Judge and the baby?"

"Why, take them along with us!" Ruth was always ingenious, and she had plans for every occasion.

"I think we might take a ride in the closets."

"What!" exclaimed Mrs. "Judge."

"I am going to hitch up the closets and have a procession," exclaimed Ruth. "You leave it to me and it'll come out all right. I'll call the cat and the goat and 'Turk,' and tell them to get out the bicycles and fasten them to the closets, all in a row, and then they shall take us to ride." On any other occasion or under other circumstances this would have appeared a curious arrangement, but to-night it was quite in keeping with all that had happened.

"Here Billy, Billy, Billy, Turk, Turk, come Kitty, come Kitty," cried Ruth; and the goat appeared on the minute, and with him Satan the black cat and with him "Turk," the bird-dog. "You must hitch up the bicycles, and hitch on the closets, and take us a-riding," ordered Ruth. Now, Billy was an obliging goat, although his taste was not of the best; for when one of the neighbors died, and crape and flowers were hung on the front door, he went over and climbed up to the interesting objects, and ate both the cloth and the wreath. He lacked taste, but he did enjoy running up and down the street. Satan, the black cat, was very fond of Ruth, and would do anything she told him when he didn't want to do anything else, and he knew what she was talking about. Turk was always on hand ready for a frolic.

So Billy, Satan, and Turk got the bicycles fastened together; and then Ruth called out the names of the closets, beginning with the very smallest in the house. The goat and the cat took a spool of red cotton-thread, and tied all the closets in a row or a tow (just as you see boats in a row and a tow when a tug pulls them up the river). When all was ready, Billy and Satan and Turk took their places at the head of the procession, and stood waiting for their passengers.

"I think we had better put the baby in the first closet," said Ruth. "That is the smallest, you know, and he will fit in like a bug in a rug."

"What have you got to put around him?" inquired the lady. There had been a slight fall of snow in the evening, and then it had turned cold. "I'm afraid he will get chilly, you know."

"Oh! I'll wrap him up in an envelope. Paper is very warm, I've heard. I'll just put him into the envelope, and then cut two holes for his eyes, and then seal him up like a letter." So the "Little Judge" was fixed. But it occurred to Mr. Judge at this point that his wife was not prepared for winter. She was a delicate person, and she wore the same clothes that she had on when her portrait was painted. The cap with frilled border was very pretty, but it was not warm.

"My dear," said the Judge to his wife, "you are not properly clad for a ride."

"I've got plenty of clothes and things in my pocket," said Ruth. "Now, here is a nice postage-stamp with a picture of the queen upon it. That will do for a bonnet. I'll stick it on tight." And she did. "Here is a lot of red crinkly paper that we use to make lampshades. I'll do her up like a bundle from the store. There, doesn't she look well?" And the child wound the bright paper all about the matronly form of Mrs. "Judge," and fastening it under her chin with a big safety pin, stood off and admired the brilliant result. "There won't any cold creep in through that red stuff," exclaimed Ruth. "Isn't she pretty?" But the Judge only smiled and looked interested.

"Now you must be fixed," and Ruth turned toward the Judge. "I'll tie this handkerchief over your head, and use a piece of red thread for a muffler. And here is a nice white canton-flannel bag in my pocket that Herbert has used for his marbles. You jump into that, and I'll tie you up."

"But how shall we get down into the closets?" The Judge seemed perplexed.

"Fall down, of course," exclaimed the child. "And I'm going to wear mother's feather-bed. Then, if it 'thunders and lightens' I won't be afraid." So at length everything was ready, and they stood on the weight of the clock, and went down to the door which swung open into the west parlor; and then they tumbled out into the room, and made their way to the front piazza like boys engaged in a bag-race. And there before the house stood the procession of the closets.

"What's become of the old portico?" asked the lady. "You must have made it into this long sitting-place." She glanced up and down the roomy piazza. "What color do you call this?" she asked, referring to the brown paint upon the house. "We always had it white."

"This color doesn't show the dirt," said Ruth.

"All the dust of the town flies this way, mother says." At that moment there was a rumbling, hissing, and flashing in the distance. The house shook and the sky brightened. Was it an earthquake, or what?

"My dear," whispered Mrs. "Judge," "I feel a little timid. I think it's because I've been in the picture so long. I'm shaking all over. It seems to me as if something dreadful was going to happen. What is that awful noise; and I see strange flames of pale blue light shoot into the sky."

"Oh, don't be scared!" said Ruth; "that's nothing but the trolley. See, there it comes!" Down the street towards them swept a thing of light, shaking the very earth beneath, and speeding past into the night like some meteor. It was several seconds before the lady was able to speak.

"Child, what did you say it was?" and she trembled with fright.

"Why, it's the trolley-car. We ride on it. It runs by electricity, the same as lightning." And

Ruth popped her head in and out of the feather-bed as she replied, the feathers sticking to her hair and fluttering about her face in a most comical way.

"I think we'd better start before another car comes, for Billy and Satan might run away. Sometimes they're afraid."

"Yes, let us get right into our places," said the Judge, who was sorry to see his wife distressed. So the baby rolled into the little closet next to the seven bicycles, and Ruth jumped into the next one, and the Judge and his wife shuffled into the third.

"I think we must make a real funny show," exclaimed Ruth, as she lifted her head out of the feathers again, and gave orders to Billy and Satan and Turk.

"Get up there, boys!" she said to this remarkable team. And then they were all in motion, — the billy-goat and the black cat and the dog, the seven bicycles, the little closet with the baby in the blue envelope, the second closet with Ruth in a feather-bed, the third closet with the Judge in a white flannel-bag and a handkerchief over his head, and Mrs. "Judge," done up in red paper, wearing a postage stamp for a bonnet, followed by fifty-seven closets of all shapes, sizes, patterns, conditions.

There was a banging of wood, a slamming of doors, a creaking of windows, a dancing of shoes, a rattling of dishes, a rustling of clothes (starched clothes), a fluttering of sermons, a pounding of pots and kettles and pans, a rolling about of fruit glasses and jelly jars and canned food, a falling of hams, and a rising of flour, and a decline in vegetables simply frightful.

" This is a very fine road," observed the Judge. "It's just as smooth as a floor. What an improvement over the roads in our day ! "

" Yes," answered Ruth as she peered out from her feathers, " we are very proud of our roads. They are — what is it you call them ? Adam, cadam, oh ! I've got it now, macadam roads. They cost thousands of dollars. But we've some very good men in town, just the kind you are, I suppose, and they've given us miles and miles of it. You ought to see how we skim along the road now on a bicycle. It would fairly make your head swim."

" My head does swim," whispered Mrs. "Judge." " It's so long since I took a ride in the fresh air, and I've staid such a time in the picture and become so stiff, that the motion makes me dizzy. I think we'd better stop for a few minutes."

" What is this ? " exclaimed the Judge. They

had gone only to the corner of the Green. There
was a very thin covering of fluffy snow on the
ground. Suddenly the clouds broke away, and the
moon flooded the scene with light. And there,
standing distinct and stately against the black background, glistening and shimmering in the mild ra-
diance, was the church.

"Where is the old meeting-house?" and the
Judge rubbed his eyes, and got the handkerchief
loose upon his head; and Mrs. "Judge" in her agitation dislocated the postage-stamp that served for
a bonnet so that she felt a cold draught in her
left ear.

"Why, Judge, we aren't here, are we? We must
be somewhere else." Then Ruth uncovered her
head, and let a few feathers fly back in the face of
her guest and laughed merrily.

"That's the new church. Our new stone church.
Isn't it lovely? Did you ever see anything like
it? Whoa, Billy and Satan and Turk! Wait a
minute! We want to take a look at things."

"You don't mean to say you have another

meeting-house, do you? What's become of the old
one?"

"Oh! that was set on fire. You ought to've
seen it burn. Father said it was the saddest, beau-
tifulest sight he ever saw. It was like a church
built of fire; and it blazed away,—walls, roof, floor,
all glorious without and within, and then it was
caught up into heaven, so father says. It made us
think of Elijah going up in his flaming chariot.
And then we built this stone church. Don't you
like it? Why, of course you do; why, I heard
father * say that you wanted a stone church, and
gave something for one."

" Like it, child, of course we like it! And we did
want a stone church, and we tried to get the folks
to build one, but they thought they weren't rich
enough. Like it! why this is one of the happiest
moments of my life. What a striking building it
is!"

" Yes; and there is some of your money in it, for
I've heard father say so. They got pay for the old
church when it burned, and that went right into the

new. And it was an English company that had to pay the insurance; and folks said it was no more than right that the English should pay it, for they burned down the one in 1779 when they burnt up the town, you know."

"You know a great deal about history and things, don't you?" It was Mrs. "Judge" that made the pleasing remark.

"Yes, I know many things. It's because I ask so many questions, I suppose. But mother says I lack 'capacity.' I don't know what she means; it's something dreadful, I suppose. Perhaps I'll make it up when I get big. Wouldn't you like to stop at the church and go inside? I've got a key right here in my pocket. Samuel and I carry keys to about everything."

"I think we might take a little rest here," said the Judge. "Do you think the team will stand?" And his eyes twinkled curiously as he looked out upon Billy and Satan and Turk.

"Oh, yes! they'll be all right. If they get tired of waiting they can take a short run on the

bicycles.　Go up there to the front door.　'Whoa!'"
This was said to the team.　When they came to
a stop Ruth tumbled out first, then the Judge and
his lady followed, scuffing along as best they could.
They unlocked the door; and Ruth rolled back to

the first closet, picked up the envelope with the
baby in it, tucked him into the feather-bed by
her side, and returned to the vestibule.　They
observed that the church was all lighted and
warm.　So Ruth slipped off the feather-bed, al-

though a thousand feathers stuck to her, making
the child appear like a new kind of overgrown
fowl. The Judge took the baby on his arm, for
he had also slipped out of Herbert's marble bag,
and then Ruth led them through the building.
Every part was explained, — the windows, the
organ, the gaslights, the carved pillars, the glass
screen, the chapel, the piano, the library, the parlor,
the furnaces; everything was noted.

"Why, how lovely it is to be warm in meeting,"
said Mrs. "Judge." "You know we used to have
foot-stoves, or hot baked potatoes, or a piece of
stone. That was all."

"You don't mean to say that they gave you hot
baked potatoes with butter in meeting, and that
was the way you kept warm?"

"Oh, we didn't eat them!" interrupted Mrs.
"Judge." "We held them in our hands, or put
them to our feet. But the little stoves were
better. And then finally we had stoves, big stoves,
in the meeting-house. I thought I should faint
dead away when they first used them. It seemed

to me so hot and stuffy in the room. And then
I remember that my husband laughed at me when
I drove home (I always had to ride, child; I wasn't
able to walk so far for many years); for he said
there hadn't been any fires kindled yet in the new
stoves. But I got used to them after a time, and
they were real comfortable. But I should certainly faint away to see the heat coming right up
out of the floor, and think that underneath me
was a raging fire."

"Why that's the way we warm the parsonage,"
said Ruth. "Didn't you see the registers?"

"Have you got one of those fires in the cellar?"
asked Mrs. "Judge."

"Dear me, Judge, I shall never feel safe again
so long as we hang on the east parlor wall. Why,
we shall be liable to burn up any moment. Think
of having one of those awful things, full of fire,
right under your feet. I'm so sorry that I know
anything about it."

"Oh, you'll get used to it! You have got used
to it, haven't you? There has been a furnace in

the parsonage ever so many years." They were all seated in the minister's pew in church at this time. The Judge was bowed in thought.

"He looks as if he was going to pray," whispered Ruth, somewhat awe-struck by his expression and the stillness of the place as well as the solemnity of the occasion. But it was hard for her to keep from asking questions. "Did you see the man in the moon as we came into church?" she turned to Mrs. "Judge."

"The man in the moon!" exclaimed the lady; "he's the very person that I want to speak to. I think it's years since I've seen him."

"Well, he's out to-night in great style. It must be because it's Christmas Eve. Did you hang up your stocking when you were a little girl?"

"Do what?" inquired the lady.

"Hang up your stocking, to be sure, for Santa Claus to fill it with presents." The Judge's wife looked with astonishment upon the child by her side. It was impossible for her to imagine what was meant.

"I never heard of such a thing," she replied. Then Ruth enlightened her.

"You know that Jesus was born on the twenty-fifth of December?"

"Yes, my child."

"And you know God gave him to the world?"

"Yes."

"Well, don't you think it's nice for us to give things to each other on that day? and don't you believe that Santa Claus comes down the chimney and brings us lots of presents?"

"Why, I never thought of it." And the dear old lady began to think a good deal about it.

"We keep it right here in church too. We have a Christmas-tree, and sing carols, and all the children get presents and candy, and ever so many nice things; and everybody is just as happy as can be. Don't you think that is a nice way to remember the coming of Jesus and God's gift to all of us?"

"Well! well! well! and so to-night is the very night, is it? Judge, did you know that our folks now keep Christmas in their churches and their homes? Do you think there is any sin in it?" He was startled out of his reverie by the question, and Ruth was obliged to explain to him what she had said to his wife. Then he thought upon it for a little time, and replied to Mrs. "Judge." It pleased him. He wished to see what it was like. "Why, I think, my dear, that it might be made a very happy, helpful festival. Why couldn't we have one over at the house to-night?"

"We are going to have one there in the morning," exclaimed Ruth. "We all get up bright and early, and our stockings are filled, and there is a little tree, and candles, and oranges, and shiny balls, and beautiful things; and we dance around, and sing, and have oh! such a happy, happy time. I wish you would stay and see it."

"My dear," the Judge was now speaking to his wife, "don't you think you could get up a little party for the children to-night? We can't stay until morning, you know. We must go back into the pictures. And the east wind may rise at any hour."

"Judge, I'll step out a moment and speak with the man in the moon. He's out to-night, Ruth says, and perhaps we can arrange something. I'll be back very soon." So she walked down the aisle, and passed into the vestibule with all the liveliness of a young dame.

"I think this must be the very spot where I used to sit in the meeting." The Judge was talking to himself as much as to Ruth. "I wonder what they did with the old box pew that belonged to me? How times have changed! But this is very rich and dignified, and satisfies me."

As this was said he surveyed the chaste and elegant interior with approving eye. "I am glad to see it. But I wish it had been in my day. There are some ideas that I should like to have embodied in stone on this spot. Strange world this." And then he bowed his head in thought again.

"I'm going to meet Mrs. 'Judge,'" said Ruth, "unless you will stand up and make a speech to me. Do you think you are as good and wise and great as people say? I've heard father tell how you could speak better'n any minister or lawyer in New England. Could you? Because I'd like to hear you if you could." The Judge blushed to hear such praise.

"I'm out of practice," he replied. "I believe my voice has lost itself. It's very trying on the vocal organs to hang in a picture for a hundred years or so. But I will say a few words." Then the Judge walked up into the pulpit, made a very graceful bow, and began to recite psalms. His voice was remarkably rich and sympathetic. He put so much soul into the words that Ruth

sat perfectly still, a thing she had never been
known to do before in all her life. Had it not
been for the floating about of feathers as she
breathed, and drove them hither and thither, she
would have appeared like one dead. When the
Judge finished he came down from the pulpit,
and Ruth was so overcome that she didn't say
one word for as much as a minute and one half.
Then the spell was broken. Mrs. "Judge" came
hastily in, saying that she was ready to go, and
the team had just returned from their run on
the bicycles; then they all came out of church,
and the organ played, and the bell rang, and the
gas fixtures jingled, and when the company was
fixed in their closets they continued on the ride.

"Did you see the man in the moon?" inquired
Ruth.

"Oh, yes!" replied Mrs. "Judge"; "I've made
all the arrangements; and when we get back the
house will be ready, and we'll wake up the children, and it will be our first real Christmas party.
I am going to invite only the closets and the

children. I want to get the closets all filled up
again for once; and then I want to see every
one of you children so full of happiness that

you'll run over and make other people happy
too."

As they were passing the Town Hall the Judge
was again reminded of old times; for that was

the very place where he had argued many of his cases, and won some of his greatest victories.

"My dear," he said, "I could almost imagine we were set back to the War of 1812, and I was going over to the Court House to express my views to our citizens."

"It looks as though they'd done something to the building," remarked the lady. "How they change everything these days!" And then they swung down Beach Lane, and came to the old cemetery.

"Look at that!" exclaimed Ruth. "Isn't it fine?" She referred to the thick, solid, stone wall enclosing the grounds, and the beautiful lich-gate that stood over the entrance.

"We're right up to the times here," continued the child. "The Daughters of the American. Revolution and some of our ladies did that. We can sit on those stone seats hot summer days, and it's just as cool as cool can be. And it's such a nice place to play 'hide-and-seek' behind the grave-stones and the wall among the trees."

"Now, this is what I love to see," observed the Judge. "This shows the true spirit of reverence. I am proud of these good Daughters. What did you say they were called? Daughters of the American Revolution? Why, they must all be dead by this time."

"Oh, no!" explained Ruth; "these are their daughter's daughters, you know. And they have such good times. Why, mother is going to their meetings a good deal of the time. They talk about the Revolution and things, and wear flags and pins, and have refreshments and papers, and elect officers, and get up plays, and go to Washington, and keep inviting each other somewhere, and all the while say ever so much about Washington's Birthday and the Fourth of July and the Battle of Lexington. Why, we children know so much about history that it seems sometimes as if we'd lived all through the whole fight, and seen the town burned, and helped drive the British away. Don't you think we're smart?"

"I shall have to be very careful how I talk

about these things, or you will catch me in some mistake, I suppose." The Judge looked serious, but there was that funny twinkle in his eyes. "Suppose we now drive around the new cemetery, and see if everything is as trim and neat there. We'd like to look at our own graves, and see how things are."

"Well, I think that's a very unpleasant way to spend Christmas Eve; and I'm sure that Billy and Satan and Turk will be afraid to go into that place, and so shall I; and you can't see much from the road; so let's drive up to Round Hill, and watch for Santa Claus."

"Oh! just as you please," continued the Judge. "This is your circus, not mine." And he smiled indulgently upon Ruth. So they turned about on the Beach Road, and slipped up to Round Hill. While they were viewing the scenery, the man in the moon winked at Mrs. "Judge," as much as to say that the house was all ready, and it was time for the party to return.

IV.

THE PARTY WITH SUPPER FOR SEVENTEEN, AND TOASTS WITH A TOASTING-FORK.

IV.

The Party with Supper for Seventeen, and Toasts with a Toasting-Fork.

HEN they returned to the parsonage, Billy unhitched himself and opened the front door. The Judge and his wife with Ruth and the baby hastened into the warm rooms as fast as the feather-bed, the white flannel bag, the blue envelope, and the red paper would permit them.

"Why, what a change there is here!" exclaimed Ruth. "It must be exactly as you used to have it."

"Yes," replied Mrs. "Judge"; "I told the man in the moon to make things look natural. This seems really like coming home. I feel very much as I did whenever I drove down to New York, and came back to the dear house. It is so nice to see these beautiful carpets again, and the same chairs and tables and sofas; the very damask curtains I made; my little sewing-stand; the clock right there in its place near my bedroom door; and there is the refrigerator. I always had it stand in my bedroom, you know. That made it very convenient. And I kept all the stores in" —

"Me," groaned Darkest Africa, who still remained in front of the house awaiting the orders of Ruth.

"Yes, in you," continued Mrs. "Judge"; "and I expect to see you very happy again to-night. I never kept Christmas. We didn't approve of such things when I was a child." She was now talking to Ruth. "But if they have a Christmas-tree in the meeting-house, and the minister thinks it's all right, it must be so. I am really quite glad to get up a party to-night. I shall have it to think about when I go back into the picture. And that reminds me, child, that I want you to come into the parlor very often and speak to me. It's very very lonely staying there day and night, summer and winter, year in and year out. Why don't you ask the Judge and me to play church with you and the rest of the children some of the times when you come into the parlor?"

"Why, I never thought of that!" exclaimed Ruth. "I'll do it the very next time (which will be Sunday, I suppose) that we have church again." By this time they had taken their wraps off and put them up. That is to say, Ruth got out of the feather-bed, and had Turk carry it up-stairs, while she took the handkerchief and the marble-bag off from the Judge, and the post-age-stamp and the red .crinkly paper off from Mrs. "Judge," and put these things in her pocket. Then they all went into the lady's chamber, and took the baby out of the envelope, laying him on the bed, and covering him with a soap-dish and a hair-brush to keep him warm, for he had gone to sleep.

"Now we must get ready for the party," said

Ruth, "and then I'll call the children and dress them. But, dear me! what will you and the Judge wear? We've got tired of seeing you in the same clothes all the time. Oh, I'll tell you! Let's play dress up just as we children do, and then I can fix you out in fine style."

"Just as you say, child. It's your party, and you can do much as you please. And the truth is that I am pretty tired of wearing the same clothes all these many years. I don't think it makes so much difference to a man. But we women like to have something new once in a while, say once in fifty or seventy-five years."

"Oh! won't it be fun?" cried Ruth. "We'll have 'Providence' come in here and show us what he's got in him. You know Providence is the big closet in the corner of the Betsey-Bartram room. Come here, Providence." This closet ambled into the bedroom, and Mrs. "Judge" took a silver candlestick with a wax candle in her hand, and stepped into the closet followed by the Judge and Ruth. What a medley of stuff they found! There were silks and satins of all colors and kinds. There was velvet and calico, lawn and broadcloth, furs and flowers, laces and linens, swallow-tail coats and fancy vests, a waterproof, a riding-habit, bicycle suits, pajamas, flags and bunting, forming an infinite assortment or mixture of everthing under the sun in the shape of dry goods.

"You don't keep an old-clothes exchange, do you, child?" asked the astonished visitor.

"Oh, no! these are mother's treasures (that's what she calls them). We get 'em when her ship comes in. It always seems to come in the night. We children have watched for it ever since we lived West and could remember. But the first we know is that mother tells us some day how the ship has come in, and another cargo has been unloaded in Providence. Then we all make a rush and overhaul the cargo; one thing fits one child, and another thing fits another child, and what doesn't fit we make over, and then we appear in our new outfits. You ought

to see us go into church a week or two after a
fresh cargo of treasures has been distributed. It's
great fun." During this talk Ruth was rum-
maging about in the trunks or on the shelves
in search of something becoming to her guests.

"I think the Judge ought to have something
solemn on, don't you?" she said, addressing his
wife. "Now, this long, black waterproof is the
thing. And he can wear Samuel's bicycle stockings and shoes. Then, here's a broad purple ribbon
for a necktie; and I'll put this ermine boa around
his neck, for don't judges sometimes wear ermine?
Doesn't he look cute?" She had helped him on
with the things while Mrs. "Judge" stood by smil-
ing her approval.

"I think this green velvet waist and this red
silk skirt will look well on you." Ruth was
speaking to the lady. "Then I'll do your hair
up with this white lace and these yellow flowers.
It's so cold I think you had better wear mittens.
I think you ought to have a train to your dress.
I'll take some safety-pins, and fasten a few yards

of this white satin on behind. Doesn't it look elegant? You must have a corsage bouquet." And she twisted up some dry grasses and pink roses, and pinned them to her belt. "And this white gauze veil will add to the effect." So it was spread over the lady's head, and fell in scant folds across her brow.

"I shall get into this pink crape," Ruth continued, "slip those muffs up my ankles, and take this black fur cape and that lovely, lovely lavender bonnet. I'm going to wear white kid gloves, and have a train of that yellow satin. Will you, please, tie this bow of nile-green velvet about my neck? And I must have a veil too. This one with little red spots like the measles all over it will suit me, I guess. There, now, don't I look just too nice for anything?" Both the Judge and his wife bowed and smiled.

"I'll put this black lace one side for the baby when he wakes up. We'll dress him up with that and some tissue paper I've got in my pocket. And now let's go and take a look at the house

again." But their talking roused the baby; so
they dressed him as Ruth had planned, winding
the paper and lace about his body as though he
were a mummy; and then they started for the
parlor, the Judge carrying his namesake on one
arm and supporting his wife on the other, with
Ruth dragging on behind, clinging to the right
hand of Mrs. "Judge."

At the foot of the stairs Ruth proposed that
she go and call all the children. For at this late
hour they had gone to bed. But the visitors
thought it better to wait.

" We must ask a few questions and find out
what the children want for Christmas," said Mrs.
"Judge." So they passed into the parlor, and sat
down on the Grecian sofa. A soft, gentle light
fell from the astral lamp and the wax candles
on the mantle-piece. The wood fire on the hearth,
the heavy damask curtains at the windows, the
rich mahogany furniture scattered about through
the room, the handsome pictures upon the walls,
gave the place a very inviting appearance.

"Now, Ruth, we're going to put something in each child's stocking." Mrs. "Judge" was speaking. "It seems to me a foolish custom, but now that you all do it we will follow suit. Tell us what to get."

"Father says there's a difference between what we want and what we need. We want a great many things, but we need only a few."

"That's sound talk," observed the Judge. "Your father must be quite a man."

"Oh!" was the reply, "he weighs almost a hundred and ninety pounds. I heard mother tell the teacher the other day that she thought I lacked capacity. I don't get along in school at all. There are so many things to do besides study that it takes all my time. I think mother would be pleased if you gave me something of the kind. That's what I need I suppose. But what I want is to know about everything. That's why I ask so many questions and tease to go all the time. I'm trying to find out things for myself. How should I learn how old a girl or a lady is if

I didn't ask? And what's my tongue for if it isn't to use in talking?"

"To be sure," replied Mrs. "Judge." "But I used my tongue for eating too, until I got into the picture. I think it's almost a hundred years since I had anything to eat."

"Mercy! aren't you hungry?" exclaimed Ruth. "But you don't look thin, and you certainly don't grow old. I've heard folks say so when they looked at your picture. 'Why, how nice and fresh and lifelike they seem.' That's what our visitors say when we take them into the parlor to see the portraits. But, dear me, we shall never get through the list if I keep on talking. I can't help talking. I seem made for it. I've heard father say that several of his family were deaf, but none of 'em were ever dumb." The Judge and his wife appeared quite interested in this lively flow of speech on the part of the child, so they nodded their heads with encouragement, and Ruth continued.

"Now, there's Helen, she's always talking about

writing a book. I think she wants to write a
book above all things. You might give her the
book she is going to write. But what she really
needs is curls. That straight black hair makes
her look horrid. I wish you'd bring her a whole
lot of curls. Isn't it queer that we can't have
a baby with curls? We've had a regular cry
over it more than once. Not a single curl in all
the fifteen. Every hair of our heads as straight
as a string. Don't you think you'd better write
the things down as I tell them to you? But
then you've got such an awful memory I suppose you can remember everything. Now, there's
Samuel. You tell him two things and father
says he's sure to forget three. Mother says if his
memory was as good as his forgetery, he'd make
something remarkable."

"I think if you will lend me a piece of paper, —
that red crinkly stuff that the baby has on, — and
a stick of candy or a poker, I will write down the
articles you mention." It was the Judge speaking.

"Why don't you take the quill and the paper that you hold in the portrait, and use them?' inquired Ruth.

"To be sure!" exclaimed the Judge. "What a bright girl you are!"

"Father doesn't think so. I don't know how many times he's said to me when I've done something queer, 'Ruth, you don't seem to have any sense.' Susie said one day, 'Well, I'll give her my two cents.' And she did, and I spent it for candy. Father would be so pleased if you gave me some sense for a Christmas present, I know." The visitors smiled as the child prattled, and let her continue without interruption.

"I know what Samuel wants. I know a lot of things he wants. Mother says he always wants to go home with the girls. But you couldn't call that a present, could you? Oh! I know one thing he wants very much. Whenever he tries to race with any of the boys, and he comes out a long way behind, he says he wants wind. Just put that down, please. But I think the thing he needs most of anything is courtesy. At least father keeps talking to him about it. If you would bring a big lot of it I'm sure we'd all be pleased. It must be something very nice, for father says something about it every day of his life." The Judge nodded his head, and wrote with his quill upon the sheet of paper. "Theodora is always wanting clothes. She's never had enough. I don't know how many times we've heard her say she had nothing to wear. And then father says she'd better go to bed. I wonder if she'll have all the clothes she wants in heaven?" Neither the Judge nor his lady ventured to answer. "What Theodora really needs, I think, is a gold spoon. Mother says she was certainly born with a gold spoon in her mouth; but the spoon has been lost, for I've never seen it, and it would be such a nice thing to give her one in its place. Or, maybe, you could bring her the very one she had when she was born. I should like to see what kind of a spoon it was." So the Judge put that down.

"It's easy enough to tell what Ethel wants. She's always talking about it. She wants some *new* clothes. She says she's sick to death of second-hand stuff. Mother's always having something made over for her or some of the younger girls. We've never seen anything real fresh and new. Father says we ought to be thankful to have clothes at all. I suppose we had. What Ethel needs is application. Her teacher says so, and so does everybody else. She doesn't stick to a thing."

"Poor child," said the Judge. "She'll have a hard time, I fear. I'll see what we can do for her."

"Now, Miriam hasn't any gumption, father says. I wonder what that is? I think that must be the thing she needs the most. She's such a chicken-hearted girl Samuel says. And that makes me think what it is Miriam always wants. She tells mother, I don't know how many times a day, that she wishes she'd have some spring chicken. You don't know how fond she is of 'em. But they're very high here, you know. And spring chickens enough to go around in such a family as ours would soon ruin us, mother says. But Ethel is so fond of them. How she wants 'em! Do you think you could fill her up for once?"

"Why, spring chickens are not in my line of treasures, my child; but I might find something that would take the place of such fowls."

"Henry says Elizabeth's a regular old goose. And Samuel calls Susie 'duckie.' I wonder if you couldn't help Grace. She needs balance, everybody says. I think she's smart enough, but she's a high-flyer. You never can tell what will happen next when she's around. Please bring some balance for a present. But what she wants is Frederick. He's the boy in the next block. I don't think it's right to think so much of boys unless they're your brothers. Elizabeth says her brothers are her bothers. And I think so too." Ruth looked very severe. The Judge simply continued his writing.

"Do you think you could bring all of us a very great deal of sweetness of disposition? I've heard so much about that thing that I'm real tired of it; but I know it would please both father and mother, for they have talked about it ever since I can remember. I know a little baby girl down South who is so sweet they call her 'Sugar.' Samuel says if we named our children as they ought to be named, some of them would be called 'Vinegar.' But he's 'funning,' I guess. Mother says his bark is always worse than his bite.

"Now, George needs heart. Samuel says George will never die of heart disease, because he hasn't any heart. He has a gun, and Elizabeth calls him Nimrod. He wants to go to war. But we're afraid he might get shot in the back. But he's a real good boy after all. I should hate to see him going around with a hole in his back." Just at this point the Judge coughed and looked queer.

"Henry is crazy about music. He wants a

violin, but mother says he needs an ear for music.
I should like to know what he'd do with a third
ear. Would you put it on the top of his head?
And he wants to sing; but, dear me, father says
he needs a voice. He has voice enough, *I* think.
You can hear him all over town. Did you write
it down?" Ruth looked keenly at the Judge as
his pen flew with the speed of a snail over the
paper.

"Yes, here it is in white and black."

"Now, William is an awfully forward boy.
He's so forward father says that he's growing
round-shouldered. He wants to be President.
That's ever since he went to the White House
with mother. It was a very cold day, the day
he went; and William had his mittens on, and
mother couldn't get to him to take 'em off when
he shook hands with the President. Neighbors
say that what he needs is training. But they
don't train now as they used to. Father says
they used to train out here on the Green several
times a year. I know the best thing you could

bring William is a training. And Susie, she wants something she hasn't got. I don't think it makes any difference what it is. Mother says if she hasn't got it she wants it. And then she snivels when she doesn't get it. I heard some one say the other day that what she needed was a spanking. But I don't think that would be a very nice present, do you?"

"Well, not for Christmas, anyway," whispered Mrs. "Judge."

" There's Nathaniel, he always wants to go somewhere. Father says that if we lived in Beersheba Nathaniel would want to move into Dan, and when he got into Dan he'd be sure to start the next day for Beersheba. He needs a good deal of watching, mother says. Samuel, Elizabeth, Helen, Henry, and Miriam have all got watches; but you see we can't all have them at once.

" Now, just look at Elizabeth. You'd think we all belonged to her, wouldn't you? She wants to *run* everything. And then she runs so much that mother says she runs down. But father says she needs experience, and then everything will come out all right. If you could bring her that ripe experience that I've heard folks talk about, I think it would make father and mother feel real pleased.

"Herbert needs backbone. I felt of his back the other day, and I didn't see but that he had just as much bone in it as the rest of the children, but father says not. Mother says you can twist him around your little finger. That would be a queer sight, wouldn't it? Herbert is always talking about a good time. That's the thing he wants. Could you bring something of that sort to him?"

"Well, my child," answered the Judge, "I am thinking about bringing a good time to every one of you. It's such a pleasure to see the old house full of children that I should like to do anything in the world possible to make them happy." When this was said Mrs. "Judge" beamed an · approval, and seemed very happy herself. "But you haven't told us what to give the baby."

"Dear me, why that's the best of all! But everybody knows what the baby ought to have. I've been a-looking to see if you've brought it along with you. When folks come to see the baby they smile and trot him on the knee and kiss him, and then say, 'I'm so glad you named him for the Judge. He was a good, great man. May his mantle fall upon his namesake.' And then they kiss him again and go away. It's your mantle that we expect you to give the baby. But you didn't bring it with you, and I'm so sorry. And it isn't in the picture either. For I've looked there a great many times. I thought maybe it was left in the house, but we never hear anything about it. Now you're right here with the baby I thought if you only had it you might give it to him at once. Could you send it to him? It must be something very fine. Even father talks about it." A tear stole down the cheek of the Judge. It was chased by another and a third. He seemed deeply moved. For the Judge was human like the rest of folks, even if he did stay a hundred years in a picture. And who does not like to be remembered with such loving words and beautiful praises? Can one help feeling kindly and grateful? The Judge's voice choked with emotion as he replied to the noble sentiments of the child. It was very hard for him to express himself.

"My little Ruth," he stooped and looked down into her face with wondrous and pathetic tenderness, "you have done me more good than all that I can do for you. These very words that you have just spoken are more precious to me than all the money in the world."

"Why, you don't mean it, do you?" interrupted the child. "I was saying what everybody says. I don't know how many times I've heard father say that your memory was a — a — a benediction, that's the word. A very big word for such a little girl as I am; but, dear me! I've heard folks use it so many times about you that I can speak it all right. It must be something very good. Why, of course, that's what they call the end of church service. I think it's the very best part of going to meeting. I always feel so happy when they come to the benediction. I think everybody else does too. And now about the mantle. Will you send it to the baby?"

"Why, Ruth, I think it must be pretty nearly worn out. Only what you say about it, and what you say others say, makes me think that perhaps it might be worth saving, so that I could give it to the baby if folks think best. I'll look it up and talk with my wife, and perhaps I'll give it to the dear little fellow. I wish it were a better mantle, however. I'd like to see him wear one more worthy than mine."

"Don't you think it's time to call the children?" said Ruth.

"Send Turk," replied the Judge, with that same funny twinkle in his eye. So Ruth took the dog, and ran up-stairs and down-stairs and in the lady's chamber, and wakened the children, telling them to hurry right down to the party.

They didn't have time to dress much. The
boys all put on their trousers and stockings and
slippers, and then they wrapped around them
whatever was most handy. Samuel wore his
father's loud, red, double gown. Henry pulled

on a canvas shooting-jacket. Herbert did himself up in a rose blanket. George had on an
afghan. Nathaniel brought with him a crazy-
quilt. William got into his mother's golf-cape.

The girls were a little more particular. They put on all their clothes except dresses. Then they wound sheets about themselves, and tied their heads up in pillow-cases. When the boys tumbled down-stairs they looked like a lot of escaped lunatics. When the girls came pushing into the parlor they made one think of ghosts.

The first thing was a walk around headed by Turk and the black cat. You couldn't fancy a more startling procession.

Then they played games, and sang songs, and told riddles, and looked for a needle in a haystack, and turned the house upside down and inside out.

The great event of the party was the supper. Mrs. "Judge" had told the man in the moon what she wished for the occasion, and while the children were rollicking in the east parlor the clock sounded out the alarm for the feast.

The Judge carried his namesake on the left arm, while his wife leaned upon his right. Ruth still kept hold of the lady's hand. The rest of the company followed in a good deal of disorder, for they were all curious to see what sort of a supper would be given them.

When they came into the west parlor or dining-room they saw a long table, but there was nothing on it. The children looked at each other and at the Judge and his wife in blank amazement. They expected to sit down to a table laden with all the goodies of the land. But there wasn't even a table-cloth before them.

The Judge took the head of the table, and his wife sat at the foot with Ruth. The baby was put in a clothes-basket, and sat on my lady's work-table by the side of the Judge. The other children took the places that were most convenient to them.

"Where's the feed?" exclaimed Ruth.

"The what?" replied Mrs. "Judge" curiously.

"Why, the things you were going to give us to eat." Just then "Dublin," the linen closet, came meandering into the room, made a bow, and emptied out a long, white, snowdrop tablecloth.

"Why, it must be that we're to set the table ourselves," cried Ruth, as she started to undo the cloth and shove it along.

"Here you give that to me, will you?" said Samuel, with a tone of authority any commanding officer in the army or navy might envy. Then he took one end of it, and Elizabeth the other, and they spread it carefully over the table.

Just then China came rattling into the room with the dishes. It was easy enough for him to get into the room; but it was quite another thing for him to move gracefully about the table, for China, you remember, was thin, long, and rather narrow. But he managed to get to the Judge, and drop a plate before him and the baby; and then he twisted around like a snake, and got down to the end of the table, and dropped a plate before Mrs. "Judge." Then he went from one child to another, and banged down a plate before each one of them. After this was done, China stepped back and stood by the side of Dublin, near the wall.

El Dorado came next. He brought the silver, and there was a fine display of it. Beautiful knives and forks and spoons for every person in the room, and ever so many little furnishings that helped to brighten the table. How these things rattled and jumped and rang as they were tumbled hither and thither into their rightful places. The children didn't have to move a hand or a finger to put them in order. Every knife, fork, spoon, salt-cellar, or other article seemed to know where to go, and got there in less time than one could say "Jack Robinson." Then the silver candlesticks from the mantle jumped over to the table, and took their places with a good deal of brightness and sprightliness.

At this point the antique sideboard stepped close up to the table, and rolled seventeen very thin cut-glass goblets upon the board. They made a right merry sound as they jingled out their Christmas greetings.

"Don't let the baby have a goblet!" shouted

Ruth. "He'd bite a piece right out of it. That's what Elizabeth did when she was a baby, mother says. Isn't it a wonder she didn't die?" But everybody was watching this extraordinary way of setting the table, so that the child's remark fell unnoticed. There was a most lively and musical ringing of bells at this stage of the table setting. Turpentine came dancing into the room. Turpentine was the closet in the Judge's study that had been used to store the church-bells in. When the last wooden meeting-house had burned they took the old bell, which rang for the last time the sad alarm of fire on the memorable night, and they sent it away to be melted up and made into five hundred little bells. There were dinner-bells and tea-bells and call-bells and sleigh-bells and play-horse bells on lines, and I don't know how many other kinds. Nearly all of these had been sold, but thirty or forty remained in the closet. Turpentine came into the room playing with these, and rolled one down in front of each person at the table.

"How would you like to have the dinner served, Ruth?" inquired Mrs. "Judge."

"Oh, served of course," she replied.

"Bells first course," shouted Samuel. The older children all snickered. "I think you ought to call Turpentine 'Bells-ze-bub!'" Samuel whispered to Helen. "See?" For by this time the children had all come to a familiar footing with their visitors, and they were expressing themselves with a good deal of freedom and having a right good time.

The Refrigerator entered the room now, and tramping heavily over to Mrs. "Judge," swung open his door, and flung gracefully upon the table a big dish of half-shells. No sooner were they placed where they belonged than they began to roll about to the different plates, like a lot of marbles, only they seemed to know how to divide themselves up so that every one had a proper share. Then the Refrigerator dumped out another large dish of something fresh and green; and this stuff sailed along the table, as one sees seaweed float back and forth on the tide.

"I know what it is. They grow down by the brook. Caresses. Aren't they nice and fresh?"

"Third course, caresses," shouted Samuel. And then he bent over and kissed the girl next to his side; the Judge kissed the baby, Ruth kissed Mrs. "Judge," and the rest of the children kissed each other.

"Awful sweet course!" exclaimed Henry. "Very much. of it makes a fellow sick."

This was followed by the entrance of the kitchen closet number one. A fine brass kettle popped out upon the table. There was a great rattling and clashing. Everybody tried to look into the bottom of it.

"That's a pretty kettle of fish," said Samuel, who was the first to get a glance at the contents. And sure enough it was; for there were seventeen tin fishes, such as you see floating around after a magnet on some basin of water at Christmas time.

"Look out for bones," cried Herbert. "What next?" And then Vanity came down-stairs, giggling and simpering, and passed something around.

"Crimps," said Ruth, "hot and steaming, straight from the irons." A very strong odor of scorched hair pervaded the room.

"Goodness me, what a treat!" exclaimed Henry. "Give 'em to the girls. They are fond of 'em." Kitchen closet number two came hurrying into the room. China rushed forward with bowls which he had borrowed from the bowling-alley; and each bowl was filled with bean porridge hot, bean porridge cold, bean porridge in the pot nine days old.

"Here comes the spring chicken!" exclaimed Herbert, as the Refrigerator distributed one spring with chicken attached.

"Do-nots for old-fashioned boys and girls," wheezed out Darkest Africa, as he pushed his way into the room. The company was getting pretty large, for all the closets had come. One stood behind each person at the table, and the other forty-three were pressing against each other, trying to see the table and hear the conversation, or do any little waiting upon the merry party.

They were all busy eating, talking, drinking,

having the best time in all the world. There was
an abundance of everything. I don't know what
all. But as the courses were brought on the Judge
and his wife became a little restless. They felt
that the east wind was rising. And when the
clock struck twelve it was necessary for them to
be back in the pictures, whether there was any east
wind or not. So there was some confusion, con-
siderable crowding, and a good deal of haste during
the latter part of the feast.

"I'm afraid the children will get dyspepsia,
Judge," observed the cautious lady. "The children are eating too fast. The closets are bringing
on too many things at a time."

"Time and tide wait for no man," replied the
Judge, who had caught the hilarity of the company, and was enjoying every moment of the fun.
"I wish to see this board cleared up before we
clear out." Now, Mrs. "Judge" was the least bit
shocked at such undignified speech on the part of
her husband. But she knew he didn't mean any
harm. He was only entering into the spirit of the

frolic. Yet she felt that he ought to set an example of sober conversation, so that they would remember him with the highest respect. The Judge, however, had a sense of humor that could not be held altogether in check.

"I think we ought to have some toasts," said Samuel. "All in favor of the nomination say, 'Dickery, dickery dock, the mouse ran up the clock, the clock ran down, the mouse came down, dickery, dickery dock;' and Samuel rose to propose the first toast. Kitchen closet number three came forward, and put into his hand a nice, big toasting-fork. Flourishing this about his head, and hitting Henry on the right ear with it, Samuel lifted a goblet filled with hot air to his lips, and proposed the health of the Judge and his wife. The applause was overwhelming. The children clapped their hands, and lifted their voices on high. The dishes jumped like mad. The bells rang so that you couldn't hear yourself think. The closets creaked and groaned, and slammed their doors, and shook their shelves, until it seemed that they must fall in pieces. The Judge gathered his waterproof about him, pulled on his necktie for a moment, cleared his throat, and then responded.

"Children and closets," he said. The children all rose and bowed, the closets all turned around twice and stood on one corner. "This is in some respects the greatest day of my life."

"You mean night, don't you, Judge?" interrupted Samuel.

"Oh! I beg pardon, night of my life. Correct, my son." He bowed good-naturedly to the critic. "We haven't stayed in those portraits on the east parlor wall for nothing all these years. We've been waiting for such a time as this. I think the east wind is rising, and soon we shall have to go back to our pictures; but I am glad to say that this is the sort of family that I always had in mind when I built this house. It's lonesome to live without children. This is a strange world. I have observed generally that the people who want children don't have them. And the people who have them don't always want them. And the

people who know the most about bringing them
up are the people who never had any, and never
lived in a family of children when they were
young. But I really believe that one never gets
much out of this world except it comes to him
through children. And now I hope that you will
be such children that when you grow to be men
and women we shall not be ashamed of you. My
wife and I expect to stay in the portraits. We
shall always be on the watch for you and sometimes in the clock. There isn't anything in the
world that would give us such pleasure as to see
you children grow and become the best men and
women in all the nation. I suppose you have
enough boys to make a foot-ball team, and enough
girls to drain a common pocket-book and spread it
all over your backs; but you are going to make
something better than idlers and spendthrifts.
Some of you will take to one thing, and some to
another, but you will all take to the right. I expect to see you filling up the house with nice
friends, going off to college, and bringing back good

company and great honors. By and by you will all settle in life, and have homes of your own; but we shall keep at home here on the wall, and look for your frequent visits. Ruth has made me very happy. I'll tell you how. She has said some of the things to me that people have said to her about me, — kind things, sweet praises, words of happy remembrance. Now, I hope that you will live and love in such a true way that when you get into a picture and stay a hundred years, and then step down and out for a little while, people will say just as noble things about you. 'Tis sweet to be remembered. And I feel very anxious to do something for all you children. This is the first time we ever kept Christmas. We're going to make you some Christmas presents. But they shall be put in your stockings."

"I'll hang up my hip boots," interrupted Samuel.

"I'll hang up my golf stockings," exclaimed Henry.

"I'll hang my trousers; and you, Elizabeth, can

hang your bicycle bloomers." The Judge smiled, and waited a moment, and then continued. "These presents are different from the ordinary gifts you receive. You'll have plenty of candy and dolls and such things. We shall give you things that you can always keep and carry with you. And they will be worth more than money, in case you use them according to directions. And remember that we give them because we have learned to love you, even if we do live in pictures, and that we expect you will honor the house, the people, and the State." The Judge swallowed a tear. "We never had boys and girls to go out into the world to make their mark. Our two boys," and here the Judge's voice was feeble and trembling, and he stopped for a moment and wiped away two or three tears, "Our boys were sick, and after quite a good many years they went away forever. Children, I want you to fill their places, and more. I expect that you will go out into the world, and do so much good, and serve your country with such zeal and wisdom, that people will by and by come here to see the house, and say, 'This is where Samuel and Henry, George or Herbert, William, Nathaniel, or the "Little Judge" lived, and were brought up.' Or 'This was the childhood home of Elizabeth, Helen, Miriam, Theodora, Grace, Ruth, Ethel, or Susie. I wonder who slept in that room, and if this was the favorite window, and which one of the family planted this shrub or vine or tree, and what was the best-loved play nook,' and all sorts of questions. Don't you think it will be nice? And then my wife and I will say, or try to say, or make them understand in some way, that you belonged to us next to belonging to your parents, and that we guarded the house day and night, for you know that in the picture we are always awake; come into the east parlor at any hour of the twenty-four and we always have our eyes open, and we know everything that is going on. We'll make them understand that a part of the love and thanks they feel belongs to us, and we shall be so happy, and when we meet again we shall have so many things to tell each other. Now Ruth will see to the presents, for we are not educated up to a belief in Santa Claus. Ruth will"—Just at this point the clock began to strike twelve.

Now, the Judge and his wife were the most polite, really the best-mannered people in all the world. But that striking of the clock seemed to knock all the manners out of them. The Judge sprang from the table quick as a flash, and in his haste turned the clothes-basket with the "Little Judge" in it bottom side up. Mrs. "Judge" jumped up as spry as a girl, and ran toward the Judge, who grabbed her by the hand, and pushed her hard against the closets in the way, and struggled to get into the hall.

There was the greatest confusion imaginable in the house. The children were all hitting the dishes, scattering the silver, overturning the goblets, tumbling over the chairs. The closets all made a rush for the door, and jammed themselves so close together that Samuel and Henry

had to raise the front windows, and jump out
on the piazza, and climb in at the parlor windows,
and the other children followed them pell-mell.
There was the greatest noise you ever heard in
a house. The clock sounded with terrific strikes.

The front door-bell, the dinner-bell, and all the
other bells rang an alarm. Things in the closets
seemed breaking themselves to pieces or going into
fits. The piano roared and shrieked like a hurri-
cane. Every board and brick and nail and bit of

glass, metal, or wood squeaked or rattled. The very carpets shook with dust and fear. And then, as the children caught a glimpse of the Judge and his wife back again in the portraits, the clock struck the twelfth stroke, the lights all went out, the children were back in bed, and silence reigned throughout the old mansion.

V.

STOCKINGS
FILLED
WITH
MUSIC,
RAINBOWS,
SENSE,
BACKBONE,
SUNSETS,
IMPULSES,
GOLD SPOON, IDEALS, SUNSHINE,
STAR, MANTLE, FLOWERS, — AND
THE LIKE QUEER STUFF.

V.

STOCKINGS FILLED WITH MUSIC, RAINBOWS, SENSE,
BACKBONE, SUNSETS, IMPULSES, GOLD SPOON,
IDEALS, SUNSHINE, STAR, MANTLE, FLOWERS,
— AND THE LIKE QUEER
STUFF.

 UTH was the only one left
awake in the house. And it
was very lonesome for her.
But she had promised to dis-
tribute the presents. Mrs.
"Judge" told her that the
man in the moon would bring them at twelve
o'clock, and that he would put them in Turpentine.

Ruth didn't like to go into the Judge's old study,
but that was where she would find Turpentine; so

she ran and got the baby, who had red hair, and served the purpose of a light, and then she bravely went into the far away part of the parsonage. She took Satan, the cat, because his eyes were like coals

of fire, and helped to drive away the darkness; and she had Turk for company's sake. The baby was soon astride his back, crowing like a good fellow.

When they got into the old study the light shone right through the door that led into Turpentine. It frightened Ruth. She thought the house might be on fire. But the door swung open of itself; and she and the baby, Satan and Turk, all entered. The little room was a blaze of glory. She had to put her hands up to her eyes and shade them, because the light was so strong. It all came from a row of packages arranged on the shelves. And

such a wonderful, mysterious, lovely sight you never saw. The packages were various shapes and sizes. They were all done up in nothing with

greatest care, and each was tied with a narrow
piece of something or other. Several packages
had strings of blue sky around them, ending in
curious bows. Three packages were tied with real
little rainbows. They were beautiful objects. The
rest of them had sunsets twisted about them,
gorgeous colors streaming from them in all directions. Do you wonder that Ruth's eyes were
dazzled?

A singular thing about the packages was, that
being done up in nothing, and bound with such
tenuous and transparent stuff as blue sky, sunsets,
and rainbows, one could see straight through these
coverings and fastenings, and gaze upon the beautiful things within. Each present had a label of
light above it. For instance, there were the shining
letters, S,A,M,U,E,L, worked upon the background
of darkness over the present for Samuel. The letters seemed to hover above the package just as you
see light hover above children's heads in some pictures of the old masters. So it was very easy for
Ruth to pick out the different gifts, and put them

where they belonged. There were seventeen of them. One for each child, one for the minister, and one for his wife.

"How nice to remember father and mother!" said Ruth to the dog, the cat, and the baby. "I never thought of that. Now, how shall I carry them?" For she felt that she would like to show them to the Judge and his wife. So she raised the window that connected this closet with the parlor, and taking each gift, carried it to the piano, and arranged the whole show where Mr. and Mrs. "Judge" might see it from the pictures. The baby, Turk, and Satan watched her while she made the change. The parlor was warm; and just as soon as she brought the marvellous presents into the room, every nook and cranny was a perfect splendor of brightness. "Dear me!" exclaimed the child, "I must go up-stairs and get some colored glasses or I shall lose my eyesight." She was gone and back again in one minute and thirteen seconds. The green goggles gave her a wise and aged appearance, and she seemed to feel

the importance of the occasion. "Here are the
presents, Judge." She was now addressing the
pictures. "They are just too sweet for anything.
How nice it is that I don't have to undo any of
them, but can look right straight through their
covers, and see what's in every package!" The
Judge and his wife were both wide awake, taking
in every word that Ruth spoke.

"Now, what is this for Samuel? A flower, I
do believe. He can wear it in his buttonhole.
Oh, how sweet and beautiful it is! The house
seems full of its sweetness. I love it." Ruth
bent over to kiss the airy, fragile thing. "Why,
here's a name under it, and a sentence. Did
you write it Judge?" And the picture seemed
to nod as much as to say "Yes." "Courtesy."
"To be worn all one's waking hours. It will
make the wearer welcome."

The next package was shaped round like a
ball. The bow on it was blue sky. "It looks
to me like a — what is it you call it, when you
look into a mirror? Oh! I've got it. It's a

reflection. Now, that must be for Helen. Yes, I see her name in fine letters of flame above. H,E,L,E,N. You didn't send the curls, did you?" Ruth looked anxiously at Mrs. "Judge." "I suppose you thought that as Helen was going to write a book she needed reflection more than the curls."

The third package was long. The thing within was long, and it looked like nothing that one had ever seen.

"What can it be?" said Ruth to herself. As she took it and felt of it, she found that it was sensitive, yet quite firm. The object was pure white, not a spot or wrinkle on it. The floating label above the package spelled out the letters H,E,R,B,E,R,T. Ruth read the name. "That can't be backbone. It's too light for that. And yet how strong it is. How in the world can he ever get that inside of him where it belongs?" The fourth package was about seven inches in length, rather narrow, and larger at one end than the other. "I do believe it's a spoon," shouted

Ruth. "It must be for Theodora. They've found her gold spoon, and sent it to her. And yet it doesn't look like gold. How funny! When I feel of it I don't feel of anything. It isn't so pretty as I thought it would be. It has a kind of dull look. But how much better one feels to hold it." Ruth had taken the curious object in her hand, and was putting it up to her lips, and going through various motions with it. "Here is some writing. The spoon is marked. What big letters they are! Theodora hasn't all those initials. C,O,N,T,E,N,T,M,E,N,T. Well, that beats me. But I suppose she'll know what it means.

The child now picked up her own present. They all seemed so bright and wonderful that she had forgotten to choose her own first. Ruth's package had a great many sides to it. Every color imaginable appeared on the surface. It was tied with several little rainbows, and there were ever so many streamers and rosettes upon it. She saw her name above; and she saw some letters printed into the leaves of the flower, for it was a lovely, shining little blossom that was contained within her package. It seemed to her that all the colors of all the rainbows in the sky had been woven into this matchless posey. There were nine leaves to it, and each leaf was made up of half a dozen shades of one or another color. And then on each leaf there was distinctly seen a letter done in diamond embroidery; so that the light which shot forth from such delicate tracery was almost as bright as the sun. One leaf had S, a second E, a third N, a fourth T, a fifth I, a sixth M, a seventh E, an eighth N, and the ninth and last T. Ruth spelled it out carefully. S,E,N,T, — here she paused and thought a moment. "Why, to be sure!" she exclaimed; "it has a very sweet scent. I think it smells quite as good as Samuel's. But I told you, you remember" (she was now addressing the pictures), "that father said I needed sense. I'm afraid he'll say that one 'sent' isn't enough." Then she continued her spelling. "I, MENT. Well, now,

isn't that queer? 'I meant.'" She repeated it
several times. "I meant cent. Were you trying
to correct me, Judge? When I said sense did
I mean (what is it they call it), oh, singular, not
plural? Everybody says I've got a great deal
of imagination, but I lack (father says sense but
that isn't what I mean now) — I lack." . . . And
then Ruth looked at the flower again; and spelled
the word, and spoke it aloud. "'SENTIMENT,'
that's it. Sentiment. I know what it is. I
shall certainly be a poet. They all say so.
Thank you, dear Judge and Mrs. 'Judge.' I'm
going to begin to-morrow and write poetry. I
feel as if I could write some now. But I must
go through the presents and put them in the
children's stockings first." So Ruth put down
her package of "Sentiment," and examined the
other gifts.

She took the one marked H,E,N,R,Y into her
hands, and the room was filled with the most
heavenly music. The package was the shape of
a cylinder. It had a transparent cylinder within

it. And this cylinder was written all over with strange characters, exactly as you see or feel on the cylinder of a graphophone. Only it didn't seem to be made of anything, and when Ruth took the object into her hands it was like holding a pinch of air. It appeared to run of its own accord. Ruth was enchanted with the melodies. They made her think of everything good " in the heavens above, and in the earth beneath, and in the waters under the earth." She was so happy that she cried. Every tear that she dropped went into the machine, and made the music all the sweeter. Then she read the words under the package. " Music in the soul; " and she felt as if it were really stealing into her, and as if it were impossible to keep it there, and she must let this music in the soul go in every direction.

" Isn't this lovely! " she exclaimed. " I never dreamed music in the soul was so sweet. Why Henry'll be the happiest boy in all the world."

Ruth then took into her hands a heart-shaped package. It was tied up with a sunset that was gorgeous with a great many shades of red. "I know what's inside that package without looking," she said. Although of course she had looked, and seen the form of the present, and noted the colors used in tying it up. "That's a heart; and it's for George. Isn't it cunning? Why, what a little thing it is? and it's soft. Will this make George soft-hearted and tender-hearted and good-hearted? I hope so. It's real nice of you to send it."

The next present was for Elizabeth. It was circular shape, like a small hoop; some parts of it were light and some dark, some very beautiful and some almost ugly. Yet the darkest, ugliest spots upon it were illuminated and glorified by brilliant flashes of what looked like lightning playing around the hoop. When Ruth held the object this singular brightness would flame up into her face. It didn't hurt. It fascinated her. She felt like sitting down and watching every change. The words underneath the circle read, "Experience is the best teacher." She spelled it out, then her eyes beamed with delight. "It's

the very thing that Elizabeth needs. I was afraid
you couldn't give it to her. I have heard it was
hard to pass on experience to other people. Now
Elizabeth can run the house and mother can travel.
That will be real jolly."

"Here is something for Susie," cried Ruth, as
she put down Elizabeth's package, and took up the
next one. "It's a cup made of — of — of — why,
isn't that queer? — made of wishes. This is the
first time I ever really saw a wish. Now, Susie
always teases for the wish-bone. And here's a
cup made, not of wish-bones, but of wishes. I wonder if she can drink out of it. She's always telling how 'thursday' she is. We're sometimes
afraid she'll drink the well dry. Why, the cup is
full of something. It sparkles. 'A Draught of
Bliss.' That's what it says under the cup. I know
what that means. It means to feel as good as
one can feel. Well, I'm glad she's going to have it.
If the cup spills over we'll catch some of the drops.
And if she feels good we'll all feel better." Thus
wisely remarked the child to the pictures.

The next package had a dream wrapped up in it. You never saw anything more curious. It was as light as a feather, as bright as a button, as sweet as a rose, as gay as a lark, as true as steel, as deep as the sea, as high as heaven, as wise as an owl, as you like it. It had all the hues of the rainbow. It was as odd as Dick's hatband. It went floating against the blue sky. It dipped down into several sunsets as you see swallows dip down or fly up when a storm is coming. It seemed well suited to Nathaniel, the humming-bird sort of a boy. And there were the letters in shotted light over against the gloom, N,A,T,H,A,N,I,E,L.

"Dear little Nathaniel," said Ruth, as she handled the dream carefully, putting it back in its wrappings of nothing, and tying it up again with blue sky, sunsets, and rainbows all mixed together. "Won't he be surprised to see a real dream, and carry it all around town to show folks. And it's a good dream, a nice dream, I know. I can tell by touching it and feeling of it all over."

The next package was a large one; and it was

for Grace, although she was not one of the largest girls. It was shaped like a triangle, and when you took hold of it the thing seemed to stretch bigger and bigger. "What can it be, I wonder," mused Ruth. And then looking keenly through the nothing that covered it, she discovered that there were a great many little, charming, luminous objects packed into the package. They were different shapes and colors and sizes. But every one of them was pleasant to the touch, alluring to the eye, and melodious to the ear. Whether each one contained a music-box or not, it was impossible to say, but strains of angelic songs kept escaping. It reminded Ruth of Henry's "Music in the Soul." Underneath the triangular box she read these words: "A fine Assortment of Generous Impulses. Warranted Pure." The big words she skipped, except the two, generous impulses. She knew them at once, for she had heard her father say a great deal on that subject.

"Judge, it's very good of you to send these

dear, blessed things to Grace. I'm perfectly sure
she'll divide up and give every one of us as many
as we like. I should think there might be a
hundred in the box. I'm a-going to climb right
up here on the piano and kiss both of you."
And she did; and she carried the generous impulses with her when she did it.

When Ruth jumped down on the floor again she
examined Miriam's package. It held a star, a
real star. The man in the moon brought it down
from the sky.

"Isn't this wonderful beyond anything!" exclaimed the child. "How many times we've said
'Twinkle, twinkle little star, how I wonder what
you are,' and now here you are." The little,
shrewd, cunning fellow sparkled and glistened
so that Ruth's eyes ached in spite of her green
goggles. He seemed a very intelligent creature.
He could almost talk.

"I heard father say something about plucking
the stars from heaven the other day, and then he
repeated something about the stars growing cold.

This star isn't cold, I know. And there's his name down at the bottom. 'A Star of Hope.' Hope so. Now Miriam will be proud enough. We shall see her going around with her star. I've heard about babies being born under some star or other. I see now how they could get under. Judge, will Miriam be a star herself now? Do you think she will star it? 'Star of Hope.' This beats me."

Ethel's present was next. The package was so bright that it was impossible to tell the shape of it. From every direction the light rayed forth in dazzling brilliancy.

"I'm sure it is a box of glory," cried Ruth. The writing underneath the shining, beautiful thing said "Sunshine."

"Haven't we been singing 'Rise, Shine?' How lovely it will be to have Ethel go about the house scattering sunshine! What strange stuff it is! As she said this Ruth took a handful of it out of the package and examined it very closely. "It keeps slipping out of the hands and dropping down to the floor or rising up to the wall. Dear me! how shall I get it back?" She chased it in ten ways at the same time. "But I can't catch it," she continued; "and see, there is quite as much of it left as there was in my hands and the box before it floated away. Oh! won't this be nice on rainy days? We can have the house filled with sunshine, even if it does rain, and the sky is black with clouds. I do think I never saw such elegant, wonderful presents in all my life, and I don't believe any other children in all this world ever got such things as we have for our Christmas."

The next present was for William. As Ruth looked at it she seemed lost in thought. She was studying it out. There wasn't any shape to the thing. The package itself didn't have any shape. It was a beautiful mass of light. Yet the longer you looked at it, the more lovely, attractive, and real it appeared. Finally it did take a shape; and when you made up your mind that it was round or square or octagonal or irregular or something else, the shapeliness of the thing vanished.

"I wonder if it's a thought?" the child said to herself. "I've often thought I'd like to see what a thought looks like. I hear so much about thought and thoughts, that I'm real curious. Father told mother the other day that I was a very thoughtful child. If I'm thought*ful*, seems to me I ought to see a good many or feel 'em." Then she looked down under the package, and read, "A Bundle of I,D,E,A,L,S."

"Why, I don't see any bundle," she exclaimed. But that moment the mass of light changed into strands of willowy brightness, and she could see there was a neat little bundle of these shining threads. She took the bundle into her hands and pulled out one. This first strand was straight as an arrow, and there suddenly showed itself at the bottom of it a chain of letters. The strand of splendor, in fact, appeared to grow out of these letters. They were M,A,N,L,I,N,E,S,S. The letters were made in quaint forms, and they were indescribably beautiful. Ruth pulled out another strand from the bundle. This seemed larger and more solid than the first, and quite as precious. Letters soon formed into a chain at the lower end, and these were W,O,R,T,H. She pulled out the third strand. It seemed almost alive, being in constant motion. The chain of letters beneath it was as follows : S,E,R,V,I,C,E. A fourth strand had the letters H,O,N,O,R entwined about one end. And there were many other similar strands. Ruth had on her thinking-cap (made of nothing particular, and trimmed with everything in general) all the time that she was examining them. Of a sudden the word "Ideals" struck her.

"I know now what these bright, lovely things are," she cried. "I've heard father preach about them, and he has told us children I think hundreds of times. · He says we must all have them, and have the best too. Why didn't you think of it before? Judge, you're just as good as you can be." Ruth was talking to the pictures.

"Father and mother will be very thankful that
you have brought all these into the family.   I
know what an Ideal is.   It's what you want to
be, and try to be.   Haven't I heard Samuel and
Elizabeth and the older ones talk about high
ideals?"   As she spoke she shook the radiant
little bundle, and saw all sorts of great, noble men
and fine, lovely women spring right out of the
brightness, taking form before her face and eyes.
"I do declare that looks like William."   She
was gazing at one of the tiny, luminous faces
that appeared against the shadows.   "We shall
all pop into the light like that, I expect.   That
must be what father calls attaining one's Ideal.
Isn't it grand?   Yes, there come the other children.   One springs out of one Ideal, and another
out of another.   It's just like a fairy tale.   But I
never dreamed what curious things Ideals were.
How rich we shall be?"   Then Ruth gathered
the Ideals together, and put them back where
she found them.

The next present was for her mother.   It was

resting on an air-cushion in a casket of love. It seemed to Ruth that the sun and moon and a good many stars had got into that package. It took more rainbows than you can shake a stick at to tie up the package securely, so that nothing could get to it. The present was a crown, and underneath were the words "A Mother's Jewels." There were fifteen of them, no two alike. The crown was a cloud with a silver lining. Ruth took it in her hands, and putting it on her head, felt the light running all down her head and over her face. It wasn't the least bit uncomfortable. But the top of the crown was the most wonderful. All the fifteen jewels studded it, so that, as one wore it, anybody standing by would almost think that the brightest lights in the heavens had been borrowed, and wrought into this head-dress. And each jewel had a name all about it, the letters being made of the very smallest stars that you can find out of doors. The child was too astonished and delighted to talk as she examined this gift. She put it back in its casket without one

word.   It took her breath away, so that she could-
n't say anything.

By the side of this package was one for her
father.   She was glad to turn to it, for it was not
so splendid and marvellous that it dumfounded
her.   His package had a bottle in it.

"I believe it's made of forget-me-nots," said
Ruth.   She took it into her hands, and found it was
woven like basket work, a sort of wicker bottle.
Only the stems of the plants were so intertwisted
that the blossoms all came to the outside.   But
both stems and blossoms were perfectly transparent, so you could see straight through into
the inside.   "E,S,S,E,N,C,E of C,H,E,E,R,F,U,L,-
N,E,S,S.   To be taken eternally."   This was
written beneath, and Ruth spelled the two big
words slowly.   "I know what that means," she
continued.   "The Judge is going to give father
some more sense.   For essence, of course, is only
another kind of sense.   Oh! I forgot the essence
man.   He brings us peppermint and vanilla and
cologne.   We season things, and make ourselves

smell good. Now, that's what you've sent to
father, isn't it? Essence of Cheerfulness. You
want him to season things with cheerfulness, don't
you, and make himself and all the rest of us fra-
grant? And he'll do it. He's always saying that
we ought to be cheerful. But what kind of stuff
is it?" and Ruth tipped up the bottle to taste of
its contents. She smacked her lips and beamed
with delight. "I do believe it's a spirit. Father
says, you can't see spirit but you can feel it. I
can't see anything but light in that bottle, but I
can feel something all through me. I must dance
a little, I feel so good. Oh, dear me! that's the
way people sometimes act when they've drunk
from bad bottles. But I can't help it." She
caught her skirts in each hand, and airily waltzed
up and down the room.

"I must see if the mantle is here," she suddenly
exclaimed. "How strange that I've just thought
of it!" And then she stopped to look at the
baby's present.

"It can't be that the Judge's mantle would

go into such a little package as that." So Ruth remarked as she took the tiny thing in hand. It was tied with the most brilliant sunset that eyes ever saw. The streamers attached to the bow were much bigger than the package itself. When Ruth undid it, and held the singular object before her eyes, it seemed to grow large and long. It was truly the Judge's mantle. As she shook it out, and let its folds drop down to the floor, the pictures fairly beamed with glory. "Silver threads among the gold," exclaimed the child, as the beauteous garment flashed its splendors into her eyes. For the warp was the pure gold of character, while the woof was the fine silver of influence. And they were woven into a fabric of surpassing richness. Then this matchless weaving was covered with fairest embroidery. Every color that imagination ever conceived appeared upon the garment. There was the white light of truth, the red of sacrifice, the purple of royalty, the greens of fresh life, the pink of propriety, the red that you see in a green blackberry, the blue of a minister's

Monday, and true blue, auburn from a child's head, hazel from a child's eyes, black as thunder cloud, pale as death, the lemon of lemon ice, orange from orangeade, and a great many others. And these colors were worked into words, flowers of rhetoric, scenes indeed, pictures of love, kindness, wisdom, and peace. It was also adorned with quite a number of gems of poetry, and it had a pearl of great price to fasten it at the throat.

The first thing which Ruth did was to try it on, but it dragged on the floor. It occurred to her that the baby must wait until he was grown up before it fitted him. Still, she tried it on the baby. No sooner did she wrap it around him than it seemed to shrink to his size.

"Why, we can use it for a winter coat," she said. And the "Little Judge," who had fallen asleep before the fire, where he had crawled with Turk and the cat, cooed and laughed when the mantle was wrapped about him, seeming to feel that it was the very thing that would make him happy and comfortable. All the time that Ruth

was handling the magic thing, it continued to
throw off little points of light and countless mites
of color, and these settled down on the furniture
and carpet and the curtains and the walls and

the ceiling, until the room was like a palace
studded with twinkling, shifting, radiant stars;
and every present on the piano was shining and
scattering light, the air being filled with music,
and Ruth was wild with delight and excitement.

The next thing was to carry the gifts to the

stockings where they belonged. Wherever she went, there was the brightness of noonday, so she never had a fear. Even the closet with the skeleton in it did not make her tremble. Beginning with father and mother, she visited every stocking, and put each gift in its proper place; then she carried the baby to bed, and left Turk and Satan snuggled up together in front of the fire; and then it seemed to her that she floated away in a sea of light; and then mounting upon the wings of the wind, she suddenly met the sand man who pushed her into the Land of Nod.

The last that she remembered was blue sky, gems of poetry, rainbows, shooting stars, flowers of rhetoric, strains of music, sunsets, closets, stockings, Christmas cheer, sunshine, and a great many other things, all standing around the type-writer in her father's study, telling the machine what to say, and begging that everything might be set down in a book and live forever.

E.

HAPPY DAY.

E.

HAPPY DAY.

Now, when it grew toward morning Ruth awakened first, and what did she do but jump out of bed and feel of her stocking; the thing which she found was a book, and she knew without looking into it that the book told all about the Judge and the pictures, the house and the children, and the strange things that had happened on this eventful night.

Later there was the sound of many voices, scores of "I wish you a merry Christmas," went flying through the air, carols burst upon the ear, and a whole host of happy, loving children shifted from one room to another, and finally gathered beneath the pictures of the Judge and his lady. Did the good man lift his hands in benediction? Did he beam with the joy of the Christ-life? The light was rather dim in the parlor, for it was early in the morning. But the children were constantly turning their eyes to the portraits. It seemed to them that new life throbbed within their souls, that grand purposes had been awakened, that charity and tenderness, the love of God and the love of one another, were moving to all kinds of well-doing. They felt as never before that they were living in the home of this great, good man, and that they must go forth into the world as his manly and womanly representatives. Peace not only filled the house, but it rested upon them. It was the most joyful day of all the years. Never a quarrel darkened a heart. Never a harsh word fell from any lips. Never a mean thought rose in their breasts. It was real Christmas cheer. And I believe that every child of them was made richer by the blessed presence (presents) of the Judge and his lady.

www.ingramcontent.com/pod-product-compliance
Lightning Source LLC
Chambersburg PA
CBHW030827020726
47499CB00006B/2106